A Lady at Midnight

A Lady at Midnight

Melinda Hammond

To Gill

Very Best Wishes

Melinda Hammond

ROBERT HALE · LONDON

ISBN 0 7090 7820 X

Robert Hale Limited
Clerkenwell House
Clerkenwell Green
London EC1R 0HT

2 4 6 8 10 9 7 5 3 1

Typeset in 11/15pt New Century Schoolbook
by Derek Doyle & Associates, Shaw Heath.
Printed in Great Britain by
St Edmundsbury Press Ltd, Bury St Edmunds, Suffolk.
Bound by Woolnough Bookbinding Ltd.

Chapter One

'My dear sir, pray do not tell me you are set against it! This could be Amelia's one chance of happiness!'

Mrs James Langridge raised her expressive eyes to gaze at her father-in-law while her trembling fingers clutched at a letter, which crackled as she held it against her heaving bosom. The gentleman was not impressed by this display of high drama. Arthur, ninth Baron Langridge, might be stricken in years and forced to use a stick when walking, but the eyes that gazed out from his lined face were as keen as ever, and his wits not at all impaired by age. He waved one gnarled hand at his daughter-in-law.

'Don't talk such pap, woman! If it's happiness you want for your daughter then you'd better let her marry our neighbour, who's a good, steady man, not be wanting to send her off to London.'

Mrs James Langridge relinquished her beseeching pose, saying in far more prosaic tones, 'My dear sir, I had hoped for more than to see Amelia married to Ned Crannock! Oh, I know you will not countenance a full presentation, and I agree with you that the cost would be excessive, but here, dear sir, is the answer to my prayers! This letter is from my old friend Dorothy Strickland – of course she was Dorothy Wragg when I knew her, for we went to school together. We were not the best of friends, but after I married we continued to correspond occasionally, so I know that her only daughter is but two years younger than Amelia!'

'Well, what is that to the purpose?' Lord Langridge turned away and shuffled across to the window.

With an effort Mrs Langridge curbed her irritation.

'She now resides in Town, sir, and knowing how retired we live here she has invited Amelia to stay with her for a few months, as a companion for Camilla.' She thought it prudent not to mention that her own letters had hinted at how much she would appreciate such a gesture. 'So you see, dear sir, it would throw Amelia into the way of so many eligible gentlemen.'

'So many rogues and scoundrels more like! You would do better to leave well alone, madam. The girl is happy enough here; don't be filling her head with fairy-tale romance!'

Mrs Langridge's fine eyes widened.

'My Lord, she is your heir. I do not say that she should go out of her way to find a husband, but she is already one and twenty, and I would like her to know a few more gentlemen before throwing herself away on our neighbour. Do you not wish her at least to have the chance to marry well?'

The old man did not reply but gazed silently out of the window. It overlooked the rose garden and, as he watched, his granddaughter appeared on one of the gravel paths, a heavy woollen shawl pulled around her to ward off the early March wind. She was escorted by Mr Edmund Crannock, a thick-set gentleman in a brown bag-wig and green frock-coat, whose estate lay a few miles to the east of Langridge Court. The garden was still in the grip of winter, but even so the gentleman kept stopping to inspect the bushes, and directing his companion's attention to various plants. The old man grunted: knowing Crannock's passion for horticulture he was most likely expounding on the best soil for growing roses, instead of complimenting the lady on her glowing looks. Perhaps Amelia did yearn for a little romance and adventure in her life, but in Lord Langridge's view a steady man such as Edmund Crannock would make her a much more comfortable husband.

'Sir, are you listening to me?'

Mrs Langridge's question interrupted his reverie and Lord Langridge turned away from the window.

'Oh, very well, madam. Amelia may go to London, if you can arrange it, but mark me, it shall be this one time only, and you must not be expecting me to pay for any grand come-out! I won't waste my blunt on presenting the chit when there's a perfectly good suitor here for her!'

In the rose garden, the Honourable Amelia Langridge smothered a yawn, turning her head so that the wide brim of her beaver hat concealed her actions from her escort. Edmund Crannock continued to instruct her on the different varieties of rose that could be planted in the garden until she interrupted him.

'Edmund, Mama is minded to send me to London.'

'London!'

'Mm.' Miss Langridge was pleased to have shocked him out of his usual complaisance. 'She hopes to prevail upon an old friend to take me in: I believe the lady has a daughter very much my age.'

Mr Crannock frowned.

'And – does your mama ... expect you to find a husband there?'

'Undoubtedly.' Her eyes twinkled with mischief, but the look softened as she observed her companion's troubled face. 'You need not worry, Edmund. I am not to be presented in any formal way, and I am old enough not to become readily infatuated.'

7

'It is an attempt to separate us!' declared the gentleman, and Amelia blinked at his unwonted vehemence.

'Oh I do not think so. Mama just wishes me to go about the world a little. You must agree, Edmund, that we live very retired here. We rarely go into Bath, and you are the only eligible man of my acquaintance.'

'Is that not enough?'

She smiled, and squeezed his arm.

'Mama just wants me to be sure.'

He turned to her, catching her hands between his own.

'You are such a child, Amelia, so innocent!'

'Yes, I am,' she agreed cordially. 'That is why it would be so good for me to spend a little time in London, to acquire a little town bronze!'

'But there will be men there who will dazzle you with their noble titles, their riches—'

She laughed.

'What a shallow person you think me, Edmund!'

'No, no, not shallow, but unprepared for the world.' He drew a breath, regarding her with his solemn gaze. 'Promise me one thing: when you are in London, promise me that you will accept no offers of marriage until you have come home and we have spoken again. Swear it, dearest!'

She smiled, shaking her head at him.

'Very well, Edmund, I promise. Although I think it unnecessary. I hope to spend a few pleasant weeks in Town, but if Mama's friend is looking for a husband for her daughter, she will not want to put me forward. I shall be there more in the role of companion. In fact,' she concluded thoughtfully, 'I doubt anyone will even notice me.'

When Mrs Langridge made Miss Camilla Strickland's acquaintance a few days later, she very soon reached the same conclusion. Mrs Strickland and her daughter arrived on a sunny spring morning and they were shown into the yellow salon where Mrs Langridge was waiting to receive them. Mrs Strickland bustled forward in a flurry of rustling green silk to greet her old school friend and such was the effusion of her greeting that Mrs Langridge did not see Camilla until her fond mama called her forward to be intro-duced. Then she could not prevent a small gasp of admiration. The young lady performed a graceful curtsy and Mrs Langridge felt her heart sinking as she beheld the petite figure before her. Miss Strickland was simply attired in a cream gown with a velvet overdress in a deep blue that accentuated the creamy tones of her flawless skin. An abun-dance of rich brown curls framed the perfect oval of her face with its straight little nose and rosebud mouth. A pair of large, dark-brown eyes completed the picture. In a failing voice Mrs Langridge bade her visitors be seated and sent the footman in search of Miss Amelia.

'I am so sorry we can do no more than break our journey here for an hour,' said Mrs Strickland, her eyes moving over the room to take in every detail of its faded glory. 'I am taking Camilla to stay with her grandmama in Bath.' She observed Miss Strickland's sulky look and gave her daughter a rueful smile. 'Something of a duty visit, is it not, my love? But let's not think of it now! My dear,' she turned back to Mrs Langridge, 'what a perfectly charming house, so rural!'

Mrs Langridge did her best to believe this was a compli-ment.

'Lord Langridge does not enjoy good health and prefers to live quietly here at Langridge Court. In fact he is today confined to his bed after a restless night. We go to Bath occa-sionally, when his doctor thinks it necessary for him to take the waters.'

'Well it would not do for us to live so far from Town,' said Mrs Strickland, smoothing out her quilted petticoat. 'There are so many amusements, especially for the young people. Which reminds me, when I told Camilla that your Amelia was about her age she was wild to meet her, weren't you, my sweet?'

Mrs Langridge looked at the beautiful Miss Strickland. Amelia had not inherited her mother's dark-eyed good looks, but Mrs Langridge had always considered her well enough, but now she realized that grey eyes and hair the colour of honey could not compare with Miss Strickland's vivid beauty. Also, although she was not shy, Amelia's nature was retiring, and Mrs Langridge found her hopes of a brilliant marriage fading: in Miss Strickland's company, Amelia would be hopelessly overshadowed. The only faint ray of hope was Amelia's added advantage of being her grandfather's sole heir, to the title as well as the property. Not that Mrs Langridge would want her daughter to do anything so ill-bred as to puff off her consequence, but a little hint here and there would not harm her case.

It was a good half-hour before Miss Langridge joined the party. She apologized prettily for her tardiness, explaining that she had been walking the dogs and had strayed into a particularly muddy field.

'I was obliged to change my dress before joining you,' she explained to Camilla, who returned an uncertain smile, as if ignorant of any such thing as mud.

Mrs Strickland engaged Amelia in conversation and Mrs Langridge felt some measure of satisfaction in the way her daughter conducted herself. At one-and-twenty she was a little older than Miss Strickland, but her poise and assured manners made her seem much more mature. She was also a considerate hostess, and did her best to include Camilla in her conversation, so that when Mrs Strickland announced it was time to leave, her daughter bent her dazzling smile upon Miss Langridge.

'Oh I am sure we are going to be such *very* good friends!'
she declared, taking her hands. 'Mama said she wanted to
invite you to join us in London, but would not do so until we
had met, and now that I *have* met you I think it the best plan
in the world! It will be such fun to have someone to go about
with. Do say that you will come and stay with us for the rest
of the year!'

Amelia laughed.

'That is very generous, Miss Strickland, but who knows,
you may well be tired of me within a month.'

'No, no, that I cannot allow! Mama, pray tell Amelia — I
may call you that, may I not? Pray tell her that she must
come and stay!'

Mrs Strickland smiled.

'We shall be delighted to have Miss Langridge with us for
as long as she wishes.' She rose and pulled on her gloves.
'There, your mama is nodding so it is agreed. Can you be
ready to travel in three weeks? Camilla is in Bath until then,
you see.'

'Perhaps we could meet,' suggested Amelia.

Mrs Strickland gave a tinkling laugh.

'Oh dear me, I doubt it! Camilla's grandmama has the
most possessive nature, and will not let the child out of her
sight for five minutes.'

'Yes, and it will be *so* tedious!' complained Camilla. 'She
will want me to fetch and carry for her, and to read to her
from the very dullest books.'

'And I myself will be going back to London in a few days,'
added Mrs Strickland. She gave an arch smile. 'Camilla's
grandmother and I can never be in the same house for long
before we start pulling caps, so it is best if I do not stay! If
Miss Langridge can be persuaded to accompany Camilla, I
shall have no qualms in letting them travel to London
together — Camilla's maid will attend them, of course, but I

shall not feel it necessary to make the journey back to Bath to fetch her. And by then we shall be into April, you see, and the weather will be better for travelling. Oh, and you need not trouble to send a maid with Miss Langridge, for one of my girls will attend her in Town.'

Mrs Langridge was all smiles. Of course Amelia would be ready to travel in three weeks, and if it would save dear Mrs Strickland making another tiring journey then so much the better.

'Well, that went off very well!' Mrs Langridge was in jovial mood when they sat down to dinner that evening. Lord Langridge had been coaxed from his chamber to join them and he now glared at his daughter-in-law.

'So you've got your way, have you?'

'Mrs Strickland has invited Amelia to stay with her,' she replied, unabashed.

'And does Amelia think this is such a high treat?' he growled.

'As a matter of fact I do. Apart from my time at school I have seen little enough of the world.'

Lord Langridge glared at her from under his shaggy brows.

'So you think you have found a bosom friend in this Strickland gal?'

'Not at all. I think she is an empty-headed little thing, whose only pleasure in life seems to be attending parties and talking to Lord this, and dancing with the Honourable Mr that, but then, she *is* amazingly beautiful, so I expect they enjoy flirting with her.'

Lord Langridge's knife clattered on to the plate and he glared across the table.

'Od's life, madam, if my granddaughter is going to look like some country dowd next to this paragon, then I won't have it – she ain't going!'

Mrs Langridge clucked, shook her head and tried with disjointed phrases to reassure him, but it was Miss Langridge's warm laugh that had most effect.

'Lord, Grandpapa, I have no wish to outshine Miss Strickland! And if I was on the catch for a husband I'd be peacocking around Bath. No, sir. I wish to acquire a little polish and to see the sights of the capital, nothing more. If you think my manners will disgrace the family name then you had best blame the expensive seminary you chose for me to attend!'

As Miss Langridge ended her blunt speech there was a momentary silence. Amelia calmly continued with her meal while her mother held her breath and waited for Lord Langridge's reaction.

'Your manners would never disgrace me, child,' he muttered, shooting a darkling sideways glance at her. 'I suppose you will be wanting at least a dozen new gowns!'

'No, sir. Mama and I have already studied the fashion plates and decided that my new apple-green brocade will suit, as well as the silk polonaise. And I will make a new petticoat for my canary silk with the ivory quilting that we bought last summer and never used.' Her grey eyes gleamed. 'I think one shopping trip to Bath will suffice.'

A flurry of activity over the next three weeks saw Miss Langridge provided with everything necessary for her stay in Town. She resisted Mrs Langridge's suggestion that she should buy a new riding habit, saying that since she did not expect to be riding in London the money would be better spent on a new bonnet and a fine lace shawl. Although she never spoke of it, Amelia was well aware that any attempt to outshine Camilla Strickland would only make her look ridiculous, and she therefore decided to keep her own rather subdued style of dress: it might not win her any suitors, but at least she would be able to wear all her gowns when she was back at Langridge Court once again.

At last the morning of her journey arrived and Miss Langridge felt a flutter of excitement as she watched the elegant travelling carriage bowling towards the house.

'Four horses!' cried Mrs Langridge. 'My dear you will be travelling to London in style!'

'I am more reassured to see the footman sitting up beside the driver,' growled my lord. 'And to be up at the crack of dawn does not suit my constitution at all!'

His granddaughter chuckled and took his arm.

'Then once we are gone you may go back to bed, Grandpapa. Come, sir, let us go outside to meet them!'

They reached the main doors just as the coach came to a stop and Miss Strickland scrambled out as soon as the steps were down, running forward to greet Miss Langridge with all the affection of a life-long friend.

'My dear Amelia, how I have been looking forward to this day! Lord but I am so tired! I had to be dragged from my bed this morning. Forgive Mama for arranging such an early start, but she is most insistent that we should not stop overnight, and this way we will be able to reach London before dark, although it will be a fearsome long journey. But at least it will give us plenty of time to get to know each other!'

Lord Langridge gave a bark of laughter

'Just such a ninny as you said,' he murmured to his grand-daughter.

Mrs Langridge stepped up hastily.

'Indeed it will, Miss Strickland. I do not think you know Lord Langridge. . . .'

She performed the introduction while Amelia's baggage was carried from the house, and Miss Langridge suggested that they should step inside out of the wind.

'Oh no, no, forgive me but we cannot stop!' cried Miss

Strickland. 'I should not have got out, only I was so excited to see you again! We are to go on just as soon as your luggage is secure. Keswick, my maid, travels with us, you see, so that Mama has seen to it there can be no objection. Is that all your luggage? Good, then we can be off.'

With another of her blinding smiles, Miss Strickland dropped a pretty curtsy to Lord Langridge before taking Amelia's arm and leading her towards the coach. A few moments later the steps were put up, the door shut and Amelia gave her mother a final, cheery wave.

'Oh dear,' murmured Mrs Langridge, as she watched the carriage disappearing through the gates. 'Perhaps I should not have pushed for this visit. After all I have not seen Dorothy Strickland for such an age, and even at school she was a selfish little thing. . . .'

'Well 'tis too late to worry now, Amelia's gone!'

'Will she be all right, do you think?'

'Aye,' growled Lord Longridge, turning to make his way indoors, 'if that empty-headed beauty don't talk her to death before they reach Newbury!'

Chapter Two

Having never been further from her home than Bath, Amelia was eager to look at the unfamiliar landscape. However, for the first part of the journey, her companion was determined to talk, and Miss Langridge found herself bombarded with questions about her family, schooling and how many servants they kept at Langridge Court.

'Is that your only house?'

'No, we have land in Derbyshire, too, and Shropshire, but I have never been there.' Amelia decided to offer more information, knowing Camilla would ask anyway. 'My father died in a hunting accident in Derbyshire when I was a baby, which gave Mama a dislike for the place, and Grandfather does not travel now.' She bent her clear gaze upon Miss Strickland. 'And what of you, have you always lived in London?'

'Oh no, we have a pretty little house in Kent, but it is let now, for Mama was determined that I should go to Town, and hiring a house is so expensive! My brother Adam is in Town too, although he has his own lodging and rarely stays with us. I think Mama would prefer him to live under her eye, for she says he is shockingly profligate—'

The maid frowned at her mistress. 'Now, Miss Camilla, give over, do. You run on so, chattering away nineteen to the dozen! You will give Miss a headache, so you will.'

Miss Strickland immediately begged pardon and promised

not to speak again until they stopped for refreshments at Reading. Miss Langridge smiled, silently doubting if her companion could maintain such a resolution, but she turned her attention to the passing countryside and was pleased that Camilla said nothing more than the odd phrase for the next hour.

As she watched the fields and hedges slipping by, Amelia wondered if her visit to London would be as pleasurable as she had at first anticipated. Within ten minutes of making Miss Strickland's acquaintance she had realized the young lady had no interest in books or music, and her only ambition was to attend as many parties as she could and to marry well. The temptation of going to London and escaping from Langridge Court for a while had been so great that Amelia had not regarded the character of her companion, but now, having been enclosed with Miss Strickland for more than two hours, she began to wonder if she had been misguided. From Camilla's artless speech she realized that the family had given up their own establishment in order to hire a house in Town. That Mrs Strickland wanted to launch her beautiful daughter into society and find her a rich husband was not in doubt, but Amelia now wondered why she had been invited to join the party. True, she provided Camilla with a useful travelling companion on the long journey from Bath to London, and if Mrs Strickland wanted a companion for her daughter in Town, Amelia was honest enough to admit that her unremarkable looks offered no competition for the beautiful Miss Strickland.

Miss Langridge faced this fact with equanimity: her object in going to London was to experience a wider society and to visit all the places of interest that such a large and important city had to offer. If there was one small corner of her mind that hoped she might find a husband she did not acknowledge it, for she was above all a sensible young lady, and knew she was fortunate to have a steady and reliable gentleman such as Edmund Crannock ready to marry her. Any thoughts that life as Mrs Crannock would be dull in the extreme she resolutely quelled, but it made her all the more resolved to enjoy her time in London.

Miss Strickland was as good as her word and with only a few stern reminders from Keswick, her maid, she remained silent until Reading, where they stopped long enough to take a little food and a cup of scalding coffee before setting off again with a new team. However, as the day went on even Miss Strickland's energy flagged and by the time they reached Maidenhead she was leaning back in her corner, petulantly demanding when they would reach London.

'Not long now, Miss,' Keswick told her in a bracing tone. 'We have changed horses for the last time, so we are on the last stage of our journey.'

'But I am so *tired* of this jolting carriage!' complained Camilla. 'Why does it take so long? Surely the coachman can make the horses go a little quicker! Keswick, put your head out of the window and tell him to go faster.'

'I fear then you would be jolted even more badly,' put in Miss Langridge, but Camilla merely pouted.

'Now Miss, you knows I can't do that,' Keswick reasoned. 'Dan Coachman knows his job, and that's to deliver you safe and sound to your mama, not to risk breaking all our necks on the road!'

'Well I think he goes slow on purpose, just to make me suffer, and so I shall tell Mama when we reach home!'

Realizing that Miss Strickland was not to be pleased, Amelia remained silent and turned once more to look out of the window. They passed through a small town and she waved to the children at the side of the road who had stopped playing to stare at the dusty carriage as it crossed the bridge. They had just reached a stretch of open ground when there was a loud crack and the coach lurched suddenly and came to a halt, tilted heavily to one side. The occupants were thrown into one corner, with Miss Langridge having the misfortune to be crushed beneath Miss Strickland and her maid. For a few moments there was confusion. Outside the coach, the driver was shouting instructions to the footman, while inside Keswick heaved herself away from the hysterical Camilla and struggled to open the door of the coach, which fell away from her. She scrambled out of the carriage and turned to address her mistress, who was crying unrestrainedly.

'It's only a broken wheel, Miss. Come, let me help you down. Come now, 'tis only a small step.'

Amelia, still trapped in the corner, gave Miss Strickland a little push.

'Stop crying, Camilla, and try to help yourself a little.'

The sharp tone had an effect. Camilla's tears subsided enough for her to be able to scramble out into the arms of her maid, who hugged and petted her, drying her tears with the corner of her neckerchief while Amelia clambered unaided from the carriage to join them at the roadside.

The coachman smiled at Miss Strickland.

'No bones broken, I hope? That's good. And the horses is all in good shape. But 'tis the wheel, Miss. Broke she is. Splintered past repair.'

Keswick had succeeded in drying her mistress's tears, but had not been able to soothe the young lady's jangled nerves, which now found some relief in anger.

'I can see that for myself, you idiot!' she berated the coachman. 'What are we to do?'

The man lifted his hat and scratched his head beneath the rough brown wig.

'Well, I do think we could get the wheel repaired at Colnebrook — that was the first of the two villages we just passed through; I believe there's a wheelwright there.'

'How long will that take?' demanded Miss Strickland.

'Well, Miss, I doubt they'd get it done today, being so late an all, but if you was to walk back to Longford, which can't be much more than a mile, you could p'raps hire a gig. . . .'

Two spots of colour flamed in Camilla's cheeks.

'A mile! How can you expect me to walk so far? I am cold and tired and I fear I am covered in bruises.' She stamped her foot. 'I will not walk a mile back to that horrid village!' Keswick eyed her mistress nervously, but before any more could be said they heard the sound of a vehicle. A light chariot was approaching at a smart pace. Observing the little group and the carriage resting at a drunken angle at the edge of the road, the driver slowed his team. He was seen to be a gentleman, his tall, curly-brimmed beaver hat and many-caped driving coat suggested a man of substance, and he had his groom sitting beside him in the open carriage.

'Is anyone hurt?' he called.

The coachman touched his hat.

'Thank you, sir, no. A broken wheel is all we have, and there's a wheelwright back in Colnebrook that will see us right.'

Amelia was standing in the shadow of the coach, her brown travelling cloak blending in with the muddied vehicle, and she was able to watch the gentleman during this exchange. He could not be called handsome, his face too lean and the lines etched on each side of his mouth indicated a life of adventure – or dissipation. But Amelia thought that his eyes held a smile, and there was no haughtiness in his manner. The gentleman's gaze had wandered briefly over the group, and Amelia was not surprised to note it was now fixed upon Miss Strickland who, despite her woes, still looked a vision of loveliness in her powder-blue travelling dress. As the gentleman drew up she had dried her tears and now she took a few paces forward and addressed the stranger in her sweet, melodious voice.

'Sir, might I enquire your destination?'

The gentleman's blue eyes looked down at her, frank admiration in his face.

'I am on my way to London, madam. Can I be of service to you?'

Miss Strickland lowered her gaze, a rosy blush tingeing her cheeks. Amelia realized with wry amusement that the gentleman was being treated to a fine display of maidenly modesty and could only marvel at her young friend's performance.

'Well, sir . . . could you . . . would you possibly be able to take me up as far as Blenheim Terrace? You see, Mama will be expecting me before dark, and if I have to walk all the way back to Longford and find a gig to hire it will make me *very* late, and Mama will worry so.'

'I can see that that would never do,' he said solemnly. 'We must avoid causing your mama unnecessary anxiety.' Watching from the shadows, Miss Langridge thought his smile predatory, and at variance with the avuncular tone of his voice. He raised his hat, displaying his own brown hair tied back with a black ribbon. 'My phaeton will seat three, if you do not object to a slight crush. Pray allow me to take up you and your maid. Blenheim Terrace is not far out of my way.' He turned to the groom. 'Wardle, you will have to stand behind.'

'Yes milord.'

'Miss!' Keswick hissed at her mistress, who was already moving towards the chaise. 'You are forgetting Miss Langridge!'

Despite this slight to herself, Amelia smiled inwardly at the look of consternation on Camilla's face. It was clear that she thought Miss Langridge could easily travel to London with the footman, but her attendant's shocked demeanour gave her pause and after a moment she turned again to the unknown gentleman.

'My maid will go with the coachman to Colnebrook and hire a carriage to bring our baggage to town, but if you have room for myself and my companion, sir, we would be most grateful.'

Again the predatory grin.

'It will be my pleasure, ma'am.'

It took a few moments for the two young ladies to climb up into the phaeton, with Miss Strickland making sure that the driver had a good view of her neat ankle as she scrambled up beside him. Amelia murmured a word of thanks to the groom as he helped her into the carriage and she made herself comfortable in the small space left for her while Miss Strickland turned her limpid gaze to the driver.

'May we know to whom we are so indebted, sir?'

He whipped up the team.

'I am Rossleigh.'

'The *Earl* of Rossleigh?' Camilla almost squealed with delight. She had lived in London long enough to know that he was the capital's most eligible batchelor.

'Yes. Now will you tell me your name?'

'Oh, yes, of course! I am Miss Camilla Strickland. We have a *large* estate in Kent, you know, but we are presently residing in London.'

'Ah, that circumstance is undoubtedly Kent's loss, Miss Strickland.'

The young lady clapped her hands.

'What a delightful thing to say to me!'

'Yes, wasn't it?'

Amelia frowned. To her mind the conversation was a little too forward for such a short acquaintance. She wondered if she should speak to Camilla but decided against it. She admitted to herself that she was no expert in the ways of society and also, from her brief acquaintance with Camilla, she did not think the young lady would take kindly to any word of censure. The evening was fine and although the open carriage exposed them to the cool spring air, Amelia had the advantage of a clear view over the hedges. Her companions continued to flirt and she was left to admire the scenery. Gradually the tidy fields and neat houses gave way to bare heath land.

'Pray my lord, where are we now?'

'This is Hounslow, Miss Strickland.'

Camilla shivered delightfully.

'Hounslow – such a dangerous place, it is not? Full of vagabonds and highwaymen.'

'You have nothing to fear, Wardle has a musket and is a fine shot – as am I.'

'Indeed, Camilla, we are more in danger of being over-turned if you continue to hold his lordship's arm so tightly.'

The disapproval in Miss Langridge's voice was evident, and drew a questioning look from the earl. Miss Strickland, however, merely laughed.

'Oh I am sure Lord Rossleigh does not object, do you, sir, not when I am so *very* fearful?'

The earl grinned. 'Not at all.'

He glanced at Amelia, and encountered such a severe look that his brows drew together. Was she, he wondered, some form of chaperon for the lovely Miss Strickland? His prac-tised eye took in the moderate bonnet and brown travelling cloak. Plain perhaps, but of impeccable cut – definitely not a servant. But Miss Strickland was talking again, and he turned back to her, whiling away the remainder of the jour-ney in agreeable dalliance.

It was almost dark when they arrived in the capital, but the light from the houses and shops that lined the route made it an easy task for Lord Rossleigh to find his way. He pulled up at Blenheim Terrace and when his groom had run to the horses' heads he jumped down, holding up his hands to help Miss Strickland to alight. As he did so the door of the house opened and Mrs Strickland appeared.

'Oh Camilla dearest! Thank heaven you are safe! I have been looking out for you for the past hour – we have been imagining *such* disasters. My child, tell me you are not hurt!'

'No of course not, Mama. We are only a little late, after all!'

While Miss Strickland explained why she had arrived home in a stranger's carriage, Lord Rossleigh reached up his hand towards Amelia.

'Pray allow me to assist you. I was concerned by your silence on the journey. Are you quite well, Miss – er—'

'Langridge,' she informed him as he helped her to alight. 'And I am quite well, thank you, but I did not think there was anything I could usefully add to your conversation with Miss Strickland.' The earl looked surprised, and she flushed. 'I am sorry, did that sound churlish? It was not meant to be. I *did* enjoy the journey, and am very grateful to you.'

She moved aside as Mrs Strickland was dragged forward to meet the earl, who refused all offers of refreshment and with a final bow to the ladies he resumed his seat in the chaise. He gathered up the reins.

'Good night, ladies.' His blue eyes rested once more on Camilla, a teasing smile curving his lips. 'Until we meet again.' Then with a word to the groom to 'Let 'em go' he set off into the darkness.

'Goodness!' declared Mrs Strickland, watching the departing carriage. 'Goodness – an earl! You clever puss, Camilla! And Miss Langridge, what an exciting start to your visit!' She ushered the young ladies into the house. 'I had supper laid out for you, but no doubt this adventure has robbed you of any desire for food.'

'Not a bit of it,' responded Amelia, untying the ribbons of her bonnet. 'We have had nothing since the light luncheon at

Reading, and I am quite famished.'

Mrs Strickland looked nonplussed but soon recovered. She ushered them into the dining-room. Miss Strickland was much too excited to eat, but Amelia enjoyed a hearty meal while Camilla told her mother all that had passed during their journey to London. She broke off as a young gentleman walked into the room, and Mrs Strickland lost no time in presenting her son to Miss Langridge.

Adam Strickland was not so dark as his sister, and of a stockier build, but it was apparent that he considered himself very much a man of fashion. He was not a tall gentleman, but what he lacked in inches Amelia thought with some amusement that he made up for in his flamboyant dress. His yellow satin coat was heavily embellished with gold lace, as was his matching waistcoat, and his tight-fitting knee-breeches were fastened with gold-coloured buttons. He carried a silver-topped cane and, as he stepped forward to greet Amelia, the silver buckles on his shoes winked in the candlelight. He made a flourishing bow.

'Miss Langridge!' He smiled at her, tucking his hat under his arm as he reached out to take her hand, pressing his lips to her fingers. 'Delighted, ma'am! You are making a long stay with us?'

'Oh we hope so, Adam.' Mrs Strickland put in, smiling at her son. 'We will be delighted to keep her just as long as *Baron* Langridge, her grandfather, can spare her.'

Mr Strickland's brows rose slightly at the mention of a title, and he made no attempt to release Amelia's hand.

'Indeed? With such a lovely visitor I am almost tempted to give up my lodgings in Half Moon Street and move back in here!' he laughed. 'Now, now, madam, you mustn't colour up so, it was only a little compliment after all! So this is your first visit to the capital, Miss Langridge?' he said, drawing her down on to a sofa.

25

'Yes sir.' She withdrew her hand from his clasp and settled herself more comfortably, increasing the gap between herself and Mr Strickland as she did so.

'Well, well, we shall be delighted to introduce you to the Ton,' he said. 'And Mama will show you how to go on, will you not, ma'am?'

'Of course, my dear, but the girls already have one new acquaintance in Town – Lord Rossleigh!' Mrs Strickland could not keep the note of triumph from her voice. 'The carriage lost a wheel just outside town, and Lord Rossleigh was so obliging as to take them up! What do you think of that, Adam?'

'Rossleigh! Why, he's as rich as Croesus, and would be an excellent match for you, Camilla.' Mr Strickland shook his head at his sister, and added a warning. 'He's been on the Town for years, though. He laughs and smiles and is agreeable to everyone, but no lady yet has been able to catch him.'

Miss Strickland smiled.

'But that was before he met me!' she purred.

Mrs Strickland clasped her hands and gave a large sigh.

'Oh my love, would it not be wonderful if he should take a fancy to you!'

'Not wonderful at all, Mama. And he *does* like me, I know it. He has said he will look out for me at Lady Oxley's rout on Tuesday.

'Never mind Tuesday, my love!' exclaimed Mrs Strickland. 'I expect him to be calling here to see you in the morning!

Alas for Mrs Strickland's hopes, the following day saw Lord Rossleigh making his way to Piccadilly. His knock upon a solid wooden door was answered promptly and soon the earl was being shown into a wainscoted bedchamber where a young man lay propped against a bank of snowy pillows in a huge canopied bed. His fair hair was cropped and one arm rested in a sling. At the sight of his visitor he grinned broadly and held out his good hand.

'Ross! You old devil, what kept you?'

'My apologies, Henry. I've been out of Town and had your message only when I returned from Ditton Park last night. How badly are you hurt?'

Lord Henry Delham pulled a face. 'Just a scratch. Felt devilish weak for a few days but I'm right as a trivet now! I shall be up and about again in no time.'

The earl leaned against one of the bedposts, fixing his keen gaze upon the invalid.

'What happened?' he asked, swinging his quizzing glass gently to and fro. 'Pudsey?'

The smile died from the young man's eyes and he scowled.

'Aye, damn him!'

'Tell me.'

Lord Delham's good hand clutched at the white sheet.

'It's Issy. He's treating her abominably, beating her. Oh she'd never say so, far too loyal a wife! I just wanted to teach him a lesson.'

Lord Rossleigh's brows lifted slightly.

'Ah? Am I to believe you have performed a service to mankind and killed the fellow?'

'No, damn you – I didn't touch him! I wish you would call him out, Ross: he's no match for you!'

'True, but if I killed him I should be forced to flee the country. I content myself by administering a thousand little pin-pricks until he can stomach no more.'

'But hell and damnation, Ross, the man's a brute!'

'He is also Lady Isabelle's husband, Henry,' the earl reminded him gently.

Lord Delham's scowl grew blacker.

'I know it! He courted and charmed her until nothing would do for Issy but to marry him!' He shook his head, a mixture of hurt and angry defiance displayed in his boyish features; then he burst out, 'But if a man can't protect his own sister!'

'You have my sympathy, Delham, but forcing a quarrel on Sir Martyn Pudsey was dangerous in the extreme.'

'But what else could I do?'

'You'd be best spiriting Isabelle away.'

'She won't leave him. She thinks he will change.'

'He won't and we must make her see that.' He leaned forward to rest a hand briefly on Lord Delham's uninjured shoulder. 'Don't fret, you young cub, I'm going to the Oxleys' rout on Tuesday night and I will talk to Lady Isabelle. Once she is safe, I will punish Pudsey for you, never fear.'

Chapter Three

'Do you think Lady Oxley will object to me being here?' Miss Langridge shook out her skirts and glanced about her at the crowded entrance hall. Mrs Strickland was busy straightening the fichu around Miss Strickland's shoulders.

'Object?' she said. 'Of course not. With the rooms so crowded she will scarcely notice another young lady! There, Camilla, that's better. Now, let me look at you . . . yes, I believe we are ready to go up. Adam, my dear, pray give Miss Langridge your arm.'

Mr Strickland promptly fell in beside Amelia and they followed Mrs Strickland and her daughter up the wide staircase to the ballroom. Amelia's polonaise gown of primrose lustring glowed in the candlelight and the gentle rustling of the silk gave her confidence. She had refused the services of my lady's coiffeuse, who had offered to dress her hair over pads. Amelia was already a good deal taller than her companions and did not feel that adding extra inches to her height would improve her appearance. Instead she wore her hair neatly dressed and with only one glossy ringlet falling to her shoulder. She also wore it unpowdered, but since Miss Strickland's brown curls were also worn *au naturel* this had caused no comment. Amelia glanced at Camilla in her floating white spider-gauze trimmed with knots of cerulean blue ribbon and put up her chin: if she was taken for a country cousin just come up to Town she did not care – in fact, it was very much the impression she wished to convey. She knew her mama was expecting great results from her visit to Town, but Miss Langridge had no wish to be regarded as a prospective bride by every bachelor in London. Her nature was reserved and although her manners were impeccable she disliked being the centre of attention. Stifling her conscience, she had lost no time in informing Mrs Strickland that she wished her visit to London to pass off quietly, and would therefore be grateful to be introduced merely as Miss Langridge, with no mention of her parentage. This approach delighted Mrs Strickland, who had been regretting her hastily issued invitation. She was more than happy to claim acquaintance with Baron Langridge of Langridge Court, but a period of reflection had shown her that, however beautiful her daughter, if she was accompanied everywhere by a future baroness it could only draw suitors away from Camilla. The knowledge that Amelia herself wanted to remain anonymous came as a pleasant surprise, and she happily agreed to Miss Langridge's request.

Almost as soon as they entered the ballroom one of Camilla's many admirers whisked her away. Mr Strickland led Amelia out for the first dance, but she showed so little inclination to respond to his fulsome compliments that when the music ended he escorted her back to Mrs Strickland and took himself off to the card-room. However, there were any number of gentlemen looking for partners and Amelia soon found herself on the dance floor again. She knew she was not the first choice of the gentleman who politely solicited her hand, but she chose to be amused by the way his eyes kept straying towards Miss Strickland. She was a little nervous at first, for she had never attended such a large ball, but she had been well taught, and soon lost her self-consciousness. Lady Oxley was a kind-hearted hostess, and learning that the young lady had just arrived in Town she was at pains to make sure she never lacked for partners. The evening was therefore well advanced when she made her way back to Mrs Strickland, who gave her a distracted smile and immediately stepped past her.

'My lord! I did not thank you properly for delivering my little Camilla to me.'

Miss Langridge blinked and turned to find Mrs Strickland beaming up at Lord Rossleigh. A faint smile was the earl's only response, so the lady tried again.

'My daughter has talked of nothing but your kindness since that night, my lord.'

'Indeed, ma'am? I am delighted I could be of service.'

With a slight bow he moved away, and Mrs Strickland watched him go with a sigh.

'Such a pleasant gentleman. What a pity Camilla was not beside me. He cannot have forgotten her! But there is time yet.' She looked at Amelia. 'My dear, how remiss of me! If I'd had my wits about me I would have recalled his lordship to his duty and he would have danced with you, I am sure.'

Amelia put up her hand, laughing.

'No, no, ma'am, I am thankful that you did not! The earl clearly does not remember me. He was far too absorbed with Camilla during the journey to London. No doubt he will seek her out before the evening is over.'

'Yes, yes, I am sure you are right. Look, there is Mrs Addison! Let us go over and I will introduce you to her: she holds the most delightful soirées and we must see if we can persuade her to send us an invitation. . . .'

Lord Rossleigh, meanwhile, made his way through the crowded rooms, nodding to acquaintances but not stopping until he came up to a diminutive lady in a round gown of mulberry silk.

'Lady Pudsey, your servant, ma'am.'

With a start the lady turned, then gave a little cry of delight as she recognized the earl.

31

'Ross! I did not look to see you here tonight.' She gave him her hands, her eyes smiling up at him from her white-painted face.

'Good evening, Isabelle. You are looking ravishing, as always, my dear.' He raised one white hand to his lips and, as he did so he glimpsed the angry red marks on her arm beneath the lace cuff. My lady quickly pulled her fingers from his grasp, laughing nervously. 'When – when did you get back to Town, my lord?'

'Two days ago. I called on Delham yesterday.'

She fixed her cornflower-blue eyes anxiously upon his face. 'H-how is he?'

'Well enough. 'Tis the merest scratch.'

'You – you know—'

'I do, my dear, but as far as I am aware no one else knows he fought your husband.'

The lady nodded, twisting her fan nervously between her fingers.

'He is such a foolish boy.'

'He is anxious for you, ma'am.'

She put out a hand as if to ward off his sympathy.

'It – it is better if he does not interfere, M-Martyn gets so angry.'

'And he takes it out on you? It would be better if you would leave him, Isabelle. Delham would take you away.'

No, no I cannot – that is. . . .'

He shook his head at her.

'You have no need to make excuses to me, Issy. I will only say that if you want to leave him, send me word and I will help you. But the very thought of it distresses you! Let us talk of something else. Tell me, what do you know of Pudsey's old valet, a man called Nathan Graby?'

Lady Isabelle frowned, and shook her head.

'Graby? I am not sure that I have ever heard the name. . . .'

'Perhaps not. I believe he left Sir Martyn's employ about

fifteen years ago. He went to live with his sister.'

Still Lady Isabelle looked blank. 'You must remember that most of Martyn's servants are not of long-standing. Only Catling, his groom, has been with him since he was a boy.'

'It is no matter, Isabelle. But perhaps now I have mentioned it you will look out for Graby's name, and let me know if you learn anything.'

'Of course, but why should it be. . . .'

Lord Rossleigh observed the lady's sudden wary expression as she looked beyond him, and he turned to find two gentlemen approaching. The first was a large gentleman somewhat older than the earl, with a powdered wig over his close-cropped fair hair. His hard eyes narrowed as he saw the earl, but he bowed with exaggerated politeness.

'My dear Lord Rossleigh! How charming to see you.'

'Sir Martyn.' The earl smiled, his good humour unimpaired by the obvious sarcasm in the other's tone, then he turned to the slender bewigged gentleman in a lavender coat standing beside Sir Martyn.

'Mr Lyddon.'

The gentleman bowed.

'Your servant, Lord Rossleigh. On your way to the card-room? I was just tellin' Pudsey there's some devilish good play to be had tonight.'

'No,' replied the earl, still smiling. 'I merely came this way to tell Lady Isabelle that I had seen her brother, and that he will be up and about again very soon.' The blue eyes rested once more upon Sir Martyn. 'The young fool got himself embroiled in a duel.'

Sir Martyn shrugged.

'As you say, a young fool. But a fortunate one, since he is still alive.'

'Fortunate too for his opponent,' drawled the earl, gently swinging his eye-glass. 'For if he had been seriously hurt I should have been obliged to act.'

Sir Martyn's smile froze. The two men stared at each other, neither of them heeding Lady Isabelle's gasp.

'Do you have a mind to play the avenging knight, Rossleigh? If so you should take care. You tried that role once before, did you not?'

The earl's lip curled.

'Then I was ill-prepared for my adversary. Now I have other, surer means to bring about a villain's ruin, including evidence of treason.'

Sir Martyn stiffened.

'By God, you have no proof, sir!' he muttered.

'By God, I shall find it!'

With a light laugh Mr Lyddon stepped forward.

'Sirs, I pray you, you are alarmin' the lady.'

Lady Isabelle flushed beneath her powder and forced a smile to her dry lips.

'In-indeed, sir, you are mistaken. I think I know my husband well enough to see when he is in one of his joking moods!' She stepped forward and placed one trembling hand upon Sir Martyn's arm. 'Come, sir, you promised me this dance, I think.'

For one anxious moment she thought he would deny her, but at last he shrugged.

'Of course, my dear.' His pale eyes rested briefly on the earl. 'One final word of advice, my lord: don't meddle in matters that don't concern you.'

The earl gave a slight laugh, his blue eyes taunting Sir Martyn.

'Oh but this matter *does* concern me, Pudsey.'

Sir Martyn shrugged.

'Then you will have to take the consequences.' With another insolent bow he led his lady away.

Mr Lyddon shook his head.

'He is a dangerous enemy, my lord.'

The earl stared after the departing couple.

'So, too am I,' he said softly. He turned to Mr Lyddon and took his arm, smiling. 'But enough of this! Come, Lyddon: take me to the card-room and let us see if the play is as good as you say!'

'Amelia, do you not dance? How dreadful for you!' Miss Strickland came up, her dark eyes sparkling. Miss Langridge smiled and shook her head at her.

'I have just this moment sat down. Lady Oxley has been most attentive and kept me well provided with dancing partners.'

'Good. Now we shall go and find Mama and – oh, wait! There is Lord Rossleigh coming out of the card-room. I must dance with him!'

'But Camilla, you can't. . . .' Amelia's protest died away. She watched as Camilla swiftly crossed the room to intercept the earl. She observed with reluctant admiration as the young lady turned to face the earl, her feigned surprise and the coquettish use of her fan as Lord Rossleigh bowed and smiled and led a triumphant Miss Strickland on to the dance floor. With a soft laugh, Amelia went in search of Mrs Strickland, who was watching her daughter with a beaming smile of satisfaction.

'She is a clever puss and no mistake! He is enchanted with her.'

'He certainly appears to be enjoying himself,' remarked Amelia, watching as the earl lowered his dark head a little to catch something Camilla was saying to him.

Mrs Strickland sighed.

'What a handsome couple they make! I cannot say I am entirely happy with this present craze for gentlemen to wear their own hair, and unpowdered too! But he would certainly be a good catch for my little girl.'

Miss Langridge watched the dancers. The earl made a striking figure in a frock coat of midnight-blue paduasoy that contrasted sharply with the snowy ruffles at his throat and wrists. She knew a moment's envy but quickly stifled it, and forced herself to attend to my lady.

'We must be careful not to seem too forward. Stay with me, Amelia. It will not do for Camilla to dance a second time with him.'

As the dance drew to a close Mrs Strickland caught her daughter's eye and indicated that she should approach. Miss Strickland spoke to the earl, and he escorted her to her mama, who put on her brightest smile.

'My, what a graceful couple you do make! But it will not do to monopolize Lord Rossleigh, Camilla, when Amelia has no partner.'

Miss Langridge felt her cheeks burn. She saw the indignation in Camilla's face and looked away, unable to bring herself to face the earl. Her cheeks grew even hotter as he invited her to stand up with him. She wanted to refuse, to run away, but Mrs Strickland answered for her.

'It is Miss Langridge who is honoured by your attention, my lord,' she gushed, giving Amelia a little push forward. 'Camilla, my love, come with me now, for there is someone I particularly want you to meet. . . .'

Blushing deeply, and furious at Mrs Strickland's machinations, Amelia accompanied the earl across the room in readiness for the next dance. He was addressing her, but she recognized the light, slightly bored tone, and knew his words were so much idle chatter, fatuous compliments designed to promote a flirtation. She stopped.

'No, no, it will not do! Pray, sir, let me go!'

Lord Rossleigh was silenced. He glanced down at the agitated figure at his side and with sudden decision he whisked her into one of the curtained alcoves that lined the room. The area was partially screened from the main ballroom and furnished with only a small table and a sofa. He obliged his partner to sit down.

'Are you ill, Miss—'

'Langridge,' she said absently. 'No, of course I am not ill, but I am mortified that you should have been forced into this invidious position!' She pulled at her fan between her agitated fingers. 'You can have no desire to dance with me, and I assure you I have no wish to engage in a flirtation with you, even if I knew how!'

The earl had seated himself beside the lady and he turned towards her, one arm resting along the back of the sofa. He frowned at her.

'Am I to believe you did not know what Mrs Strickland was about?'

Miss Langridge turned an indignant glance upon him.

'Of course not, I would never—'

'What you mean to say is that no lady of breeding would condone such forward conduct. But that would be disloyal to your hostess, would it not?'

'I have no experience of how London society conducts itself,' she said stiffly. 'And it would be most improper of me to criticize Mrs Strickland.'

'Of course it would.' He removed the fan from her fingers, flicked it open and began to wave it gently before her, cooling her heated cheeks. 'How do you come to be staying with the family?'

'Mrs Strickland and my mother are old friends. An invitation to visit London . . . but you must not think I complain, sir. I have received nothing but kindness.'

'Kindness! Would the lady have invited you, do you think, had you been a beauty, rivalling Miss Strickland? No, I can tell by your look that you know as well as I that Mrs Strickland has only one thought, to catch a husband for her daughter.'

Miss Langridge looked up at that, her eyes glinting with sparks of anger.

'And your only thought is to engage her in a heady flirtation that could well break her heart!'

A sneer lifted the corner of his mouth.

'Camilla Strickland has the soul of a courtesan! You may be sure her heart will not be touched.'

'And, of course, you would know, sir!'

'Aye, only too well!'

Amelia lifted her hand, a tiny gesture of defence. The earl's look softened. He said gently, 'Believe me, Miss Langridge, I know your friend's little game. It is played by a thousand other women here in Town.'

'Then it is all the more despicable! I had not thought to find society so shallow!'

'Did you not come here to find a husband?'

'No! I came to . . .' she broke off, sighing as she tried to put her thoughts into words. 'I want to go to concerts, and — and lectures! To see places I have only read about in books, to discuss politics and religion.'

'Then you should have chosen a different hostess.'

She hung her head. 'I know that now.'

He smiled. 'You are an unusual girl! To come all this way with no thought of marriage. Is there perhaps some gentleman at home who holds your affection?'

She thought of Edmund Crannock, dull respectable Edmund! Had she not come to London to escape him? Mistaking the smile that curved her lips, the gentleman sat back. 'Ah, so there is someone! What is he like, this paragon?'

Amelia put up her chin. Whatever her own feelings, she would defend him.

'A gentleman of learning and refinement, not a coxcomb who is easily distracted by a pretty ankle!' She met his amused look defiantly, anger overcoming her shyness. After a moment the earl laughed softly.

'He sounds like a dull dog, but if you love him!' He handed her the fan. 'Come, Miss Langridge, the dance is ending, and we must return to this shallow society before we become the latest subject of its gossip!'

He took her hand and led her back into the room. The crowd seemed even thicker, the noise greater and she was thankful for the earl's escort. He led her towards Mrs Strickland and her daughter, saying softly, 'In this crowd they will not have seen that we were not dancing. When she asks, you must tell her that I spent the whole dance talking of the lovely Camilla.'

'I shall do no such thing!'

'Will you tell her the truth then, that we spent the past half-hour enjoying a cosy *tête-à-tête*? I will own myself surprised if the mother or daughter don't scratch your eyes out for it!'

She laughed at that, and met his mocking glance with eyes brimful of merriment.

'How unkind of you to say so, even though it might be true!'

They had come up to Mrs Strickland and with an elegant bow he sauntered away, leaving the ladies to gaze after him.

'Is he not a charming man?' sighed Mrs Strickland.

Amelia chuckled. 'A nonsensical one, ma'am, but entertaining.'

Mrs Strickland looked suspiciously at her.

'My dear, pray for heaven's sake do not allow yourself to develop a *tendre* for Lord Rossleigh! He may make himself agreeable to you, but it is Camilla he wants.'

'I know that, ma'am. He – he spent the whole time talking of her!'

The next day Amelia found her good humour sorely tried as Camilla boasted of her latest conquest to anyone who would listen and by noon Amelia was yearning for a little solitude. After lunch she excused herself from joining Mrs Strickland and her daughter on a shopping trip and instead took her work box to the morning-room where she spent a pleasant hour embroidering a pair of slippers for her grandfather.

Hearing voices in the hall she assumed it was her hostess returned and began to pack away her work, but a moment later the door opened to admit Mr Adam Strickland. He was already dressed for the evening in a coat of champagne-coloured velvet, heavily laced with gold and falling open to display a matching waistcoat stretched across his stocky frame. His hair was lavishly powdered and tied at the nape of the neck with a gold ribbon. Startled, she rose to greet him as he crossed the room and bowed to her.

'Mistress Langridge, all alone, ma'am?'

'As you see, sir. Your mama and sister went shopping. I expect them at any moment.'

'Well, we will go on very well without them.' He took her hand and pressed a hot kiss on to it. 'May I sit with you?'

When she assented he pulled up a chair, so close to her own that their knees were almost touching. Amelia sought for something to say.

'Y-you are dressed very fine, Mr Strickland. Do you go to Almacks tonight?'

'No, to the theatre with a party of friends. You could come with us, Miss Langridge, only say the word!'

'Thank you sir, but it is not possible.'

'Ah, you are thinking of the proprieties – never fear, madam, a matron, Mrs Chadderton, will be in attendance.' He moved to the edge of his seat and leaned towards her. 'She is not one to be spoiling our fun, she does not object to a few ... high spirits.' He put his hand on her knee. 'What do you say, m'dear?'

Amelia pulled away. 'No, sir. I think not.'

He sat back, grinning.

'Why you are a shy little thing! But once you know me better—' He broke off as the door opened and Amelia was relieved to see Mrs Strickland enter. She swept across the room with Camilla close behind her and they were both

40

clearly big with news.

'Adam, my love, you did not say you would be here today.'

'I know, Mama, I just looked in to see if Miss Langridge would care to come to the theatre with me, but she does not think it proper.' Mr Strickland rose to receive his mama's embrace, and Amelia was glad of the diversion to recover her composure.

'I should think not, when she has known you but five minutes. But my dears,' Mrs Strickland could not be diverted from her news. 'Such a day as we have had! Camilla wanted to buy a new reticule and gloves to match her new walking gown so we had Dan Coachman take us to the Pantheon Bazaar, where we picked up the prettiest little silk purse.'

'Mama, I am sure they do not wish to hear about that.' Miss Strickland interrupted her, her eyes shining.

'Oho!' cried Mr Strickland, grinning at his sister. 'If Camilla don't want to talk about her latest trinkets there can only be one reason — a man.'

'Pray Adam, do not be so ill-bred!' cried his mother, shocked.

'And you are wrong, dear brother,' declared Camilla, looking smug. 'He is not a man, but an earl.'

'Well, an earl's sister to be precise.' Mrs Strickland corrected her. She turned to Miss Langridge, her eyes shining with triumph. 'Lady Redcliffe, no less.'

Amelia blinked. 'At the Pantheon Bazaar, ma'am?'

'No, no, not *there*. We had gone on to Bond Street, because Camilla had seen a pretty little bonnet, but in fact once she had tried it she found it did not suit after all.'

Miss Strickland stepped forward.

'Mama, can you not get to the point?' She turned to Amelia. 'As we came out of the milliners who should we see on the other side of the road but Lord Rossleigh and his sister, Lady Charlotte Redcliffe. Of course we did not know who she was *then*, but Lord Rossleigh saw us, and came over directly to make her known to us.' She looked around. 'Do you not see what an honour that was for me? To wish to present me to his sister!'

Amelia smiled, but could think of nothing to say. However, no answer was required of her for Camilla continued with barely a pause.

'Well, of course we spoke for a few moments and Lady Charlotte was most gracious, and she has invited us to her supper on Thursday.'

Mr Strickland laughed.

'Is that all? I expected at least to hear that you were betrothed to this earl of yours, Camilla.'

'All?' declared Mrs Strickland. 'Do you not realize what an honour this is? Lady Charlotte has promised to send a card for her next supper. You do not seem to realize, Adam, these invitations are not given to everyone.'

'No, and not everyone would want to attend!' retorted Mr Strickland. 'Devilish dull affairs, all rhenish and recitation. No card tables, no dancing, just poets, writers and artists.'

Mrs Strickland's face fell, but her daughter waved away these objections.

'Rossleigh must want me to be there, or why would he suggest that Lady Charlotte invite me?'

Mr Strickland shook his head.

'You won't enjoy it, Sis. It ain't at all your sort of thing.'

She gave him a saucy smile.

'Perhaps I will make it my sort of thing, if it pleases Rossleigh.'

Mr Strickland prepared to take his leave.

'Dashed if I can see why it should,' he said. 'I understand the earl rarely attends Lady Charlotte's suppers: he's more at home at the racecourse, or the gaming table. Of course he's a favourite with the ladies, but he's not one of your literary coves. I wonder that he should want you there.'

*

Lady Charlotte had expressed much the same view to her brother as they walked away from Mrs Strickland that afternoon. She cast a sly glance up at her escort.

'Well, Ross? What little game are you playing now? Miss Strickland is certainly a beauty, but hardly likely to enjoy one of my soirées.'

A ghost of a smile curved his lips.

'Indulge me, Lottie! Put the charming Miss Strickland on your guest list. And she has a companion staying with her – she had best be invited too.'

'But of course, love. When have I been able to refuse you anything?'

'You are an ideal sister, my dear. Remind me to buy you that diamond collar you admired on the way here.'

'You are too generous, my love: I am only too happy to oblige you, especially if it distracts you from your feud with Sir Martyn.'

'Nothing will do that.'

She laid a hand on his arm, suddenly serious.

'Susannah is gone, Ross. Let it rest there, or this thirst for vengeance will destroy you.'

He laughed softly.

'Devil a bit, Lottie! I live for pleasure, have you not heard?'

She sighed, knowing he would not give her a serious answer, and replied in the same bantering tone.

'Does this mean we will have the pleasure of your company on Thursday?'

'Accept my apologies now, my dear. I have other plans for Thursday evening.'

Chapter Four

*I*t was a stormy night and the little-used road to Home End turned quickly to mud. There was only one traveller on the road and he noted with relief the straggling buildings of a roadside inn. Light spilled from the windows, for the heavy rain clouds had brought an early dusk. He rode into the yard and dismounted, throwing the reins to a waiting stable boy before striding into the tap room, the rain dripping from his caped greatcoat.

Lord Rossleigh took off his sodden hat, shook it out and looked about him. The air in the low room was very warm and thick with pipe smoke, increased at intervals by an acrid cloud from the logs smouldering sullenly in the hearth. For a brief moment he thought longingly of his sister's white and gold reception rooms, where fires would be blazing merrily beneath the freshly swept chimneys for the comfort of her guests. A rotund figure in a greasy apron bustled forward, beaming.

'Evening, sir. What will be your pleasure?'

'Some of your home-brewed, landlord, and a room for the night,' returned the earl, stripping off his gloves.

'Home-brewed coming up, sir, and I'll have a chamber prepared for you. P'rhaps you'd care for a private sitting-room. . . . ?

'No, no, this suits me very well, but perhaps you could hang this somewhere to dry.' Lord Rossleigh shrugged off his greatcoat to reveal a plain coat and waistcoat, embellished

only by the snowy ruffles at his throat and wrists. The landlord took the caped greatcoat reverently and hurried away to
have the best bedchamber prepared, his guest's status in no
way diminished in his eyes by the plainness of his dress. No
one seeing the impeccable cut of that brown riding jacket and
the perfectly shaped buckskins could think their owner
anything less than a top o' the trees gentleman.

The earl went to stand before the fire, smiling affably at
the ancient occupying the settle to one side of the hearth. The
old man cast a rheumy eye over the newcomer and deigned
to give him a nod, then went back to smoking his pipe. Lord
Rossleigh stooped to pick up the poker.

'Waste o' time,' opined the ancient, watching his attempts
to coax a flame from the fire. 'Them logs is sopped through.'

'Ah.' The earl gave up and settled himself into a chair opposite the old man. 'Pity they're so damp. I like a cheerful blaze
on a wet night.'

The ancient cocked one shaggy eyebrow.

'Come far?'

My lord settled himself more comfortably in his chair.

'Far enough to be in need of a bed for the night.'

'Ah well, this'll do for 'ee then, if it's clean sheets and plain
fare you want. Nothin' fancy here at the Bell.' The old man
leaned forward to spit in the fire. 'Them as wants airs and
graces puts up at the Kings Arms.'

'But that's two miles further on, and this inn serves the
village of Home End, does it not?'

'Aye, reckon it do.'

Lord Rossleigh took his tankard from the landlord and
asked him to bring another for his new acquaintance.
Hearing this, the ancient removed his pipe from his mouth
and gave a toothless grin.

'Much obliged to 'ee, sir.'

The landlord returned with the second tankard and bustled

off again to fetch in dry logs. In a very short time the flames were dancing merrily in the fireplace while the earl and his elderly companion drank their ale and regarded the blaze with silent approval.

Lord Rossleigh drained his tankard.

'So this is the only inn in the village.'

'Ah, and it's a blessing the beer's good, though it don't be doing to tell Sam Taylor that!' the old man cackled as the landlord brought more ale to them.

'There you are, Joseph,' declared their host, holding out the brimming tankard. 'And just remember you're beholden to this gentleman, and don't be rattling on forever.'

The ancient scowled, and muttered an invective to Sam Taylor to keep to his own business and leave his customers to enjoy themselves.

'Damned upstart,' he grumbled, waving his pipe at the landlord's retreating back. 'Only moved to Home End five years ago and thinks he can tell us all what to do.'

'You have been in the village much longer then?'

'Aye, sixty years, man and boy.'

'And I don't doubt you've seen some changes here.'

'Reckon I 'ave. Not as many as up at the King's Head, of course, now that it's a main coaching route: there's houses all around it now but here at Home End, well, it's a quiet village.'

'And new faces? Apart from our host, that is.'

The old man shook his head.

'Farming families. Don't change much, except maybe to bring in a new bride. I remembers old Wilmot doing that, thirty years ago it must be. Married a Hertfordshire lass – broke a lot of hearts, he did, him being such a fine young man, and with his own farm and all.'

'No doubt his bride was exceptional.'

'Aye, she was a handsome gel, hair as red as that fire, and a temper as hot! But she's a good woman, Mrs Wilmot. Works hard and gave her man a quiverful of children to follow after 'un, as well as looking after that brother of hers.'

'Brother, you say? Does he live here with her?'

The old man took a long pull from his tankard and smacked his lips.

'No, no, Graby's got his own cottage here in the village. He was servant to some great lord, they say, though he's never spoke of it. He had an accident and broke his hip, never recovered properly, so Wilmot put him in Weir Cottage and Mrs Wilmot goes in every day to see him and take him his meals.'

'A good sister then. How long has she been doing that?'

The old man frowned.

'Oh, must be a dozen years or so.' He drained his tankard and looked at the earl so expectantly that my lord laughed and called to Master Taylor to fill 'em up again.

The next morning the earl breakfasted early and set off through the sleepy village. The rain had stopped but the earth track had not dried out and he was obliged to pick his route through the muddy ruts. He arrived at Weir Cottage to find a tidy dwelling, the weeds cleared from the path and its door freshly painted. He knocked and was about to knock again when he heard a shuffling within, and the drawing back of the bolt. An old man opened the door. He was bent over with age, but the pale eyes that regarded the earl were sharp and inquisitive. He had a shock of white hair and his skin bore the mottled-brown marks that in a young man might well have been freckles. The earl nodded to him.

'Mr Graby? Good day to you sir. I've come to talk to you about Sir Martyn Pudsey.'

The old man's eyes grew wary and he tried to shut the door, but the earl was ready for him. He had put his booted foot in the door and then added the weight of his body to force his way in.

'May I come in? Thank you.' He stepped over the threshold

as the old man backed away.

'Did – did Sir Martyn send you?' His voice was querulous with age and fear.

'No, no, and I do not mean to tell him of this visit, as long as you tell me what I want to know.' He shut the door behind him and turned to smile at his host. 'Now, sir, shall we sit down?'

Three hours later the earl rode away from the village, well pleased with the outcome of his visit. He reached Rossleigh House shortly before dinner and went up to his room, where his valet was laying out fresh clothes. The servant's disapproving look was not lost upon the earl.

'Why so severe, O'Brien?' he said, a laugh in his voice. 'I am returned safely, you see.'

'Aye, but your riding coat is ruined, my lord,' retorted the valet, helping his master to remove the offending article.

'I merely gave it to the landlord at the inn to press.'

O'Brien closed his eyes as though in acute pain.

'There is little point in employing the services of London's best tailors,' he said, at his most dignified, 'if you are going to hand over your coats to rural idiots. Why, just look at that sleeve – scorched, so it is.'

'Nonsense, man. Give it a good brushing and it will be as good as new,' retorted the earl, knowing that his servant's displeasure stemmed from the fact that he had not been allowed to accompany his master.

'And your top-boots!' exclaimed O'Brien. 'Pray don't tell me you allowed the common Boots to touch them.'

'Very well I won't,' grinned the earl. 'But never mind boots, O'Brien, I have been visiting an old man who could be very useful to me. He is not yet convinced to help us, but I have given him some time to think over my proposal.'

'Which is, my lord?'

'That if he gives me the evidence I require, he will be protected from Pudsey, and that he shall have a substantial reward for his efforts. You are not smiling, O'Brien. Do you not think Mr Graby will take my offer?'

The valet shrugged.

'It seems to me, my lord, that if this old man knows so much about Sir Martyn, he would already have been "rewarded" to keep his silence.'

'Ah, now there you have a point, O'Brien, but it seems Sir Martyn made an error of judgement with this old man. He did indeed pension him off, but he was not generous enough, and Graby is resentful of the fact that he is almost a penniless cripple.' The earl smiled, but there was no warmth in his eyes. 'I think Nathan Graby might well be the key to Pudsey's downfall.'

It was two days after Lady Charlotte's supper party that Amelia saw the earl again. She was waiting outside a fashionable milliner in Pall Mall while Mrs Strickland and her daughter were engrossed in deciding between the rival merits of a small-brimmed beaver hat and a neat cap of Italian silk when she saw Lord Rossleigh approaching in his phaeton. He noticed her and immediately drew up, much to the annoyance of a hackney carriage following closely behind him. Ignoring the shouts from the hackney driver, Lord Rossleigh jumped down from the carriage, handing the reins to his groom with instructions to take it round the block.

Conscious of the honour he was paying her, Miss Langridge lost no time in thanking him for including her in Lady Charlotte's invitation.

'For I know you must have instructed your sister to do so. How else did she know my name?'

He inclined his head.

'You are waiting for Mrs Strickland perhaps?'

'Yes sir. We have come to return a bonnet.' A mischievous

twinkle lit her eyes. 'Camilla found the ribbons were not to her taste. However, I believe she has now seen another cap that has taken her fancy. I prefer to watch the world from here than remain in a stuffy little shop.'

'Just so, madam! So you enjoyed my sister's party?'

'Very much so. There were so many interesting people there! The Thrales came with Mr Johnson (such a loud, self-important man, I thought) – and several poets brought their work along to read to us.'

'Was Mr Goldsmith there?'

'Why yes. He appeared in such a gorgeous coat; I never saw so much gold lacing before, a veritable peacock.'

'You did not like him?'

'On the contrary. I know he is thought vain, but Lady Charlotte was kind enough to introduce us and he was very generous, and talked to me for a good ten minutes. He was persuaded to read to the assembly from the *Vicar of Wakefield* and *The Deserted Village* – it was so enlightening to hear the words read as they were intended. Then later, he even gave us a snippet of a new play, *She Stoops to Conquer*.'

'And how did Miss Strickland enjoy that? The truth, Miss Langridge, if you please! You can be frank with me.'

She laughed. 'Very well sir, since you insist upon it. Poor Camilla did not enjoy it at all. I have had the benefit of many hours of solitude to fill with books, but Camilla is not widely read, you see.'

'You mean that she is a pretty little widgeon who spends all her time thinking what hat will best become her. I doubt she has a serious thought in her head. Was she thoroughly bored?'

'I am afraid so. Her brother warned her how it would be, but she insisted upon going. You see, she is unused to parties where she is not the centre of attention, surrounded by admirers who will attend her every whim.'

'Are you telling me Miss Strickland did not turn any heads? You surprise me. Even in such august company as my sister gathers, men still appreciate a pretty woman.'

'Well, of course, she attracted some attention, but when one young man tried to converse with her during Mr Johnson's readings, they were most roundly shushed! And to cap it all, you did not put in an appearance. Poor Camilla, I believe she has rarely spent a more miserable evening.'

'And you, Miss Langridge?'

'Me? I have rarely spent a more enjoyable one. The society was gay, the conversation witty and intelligent and your sister so very kind – how could I fail to enjoy myself.' She looked up at him. 'Did – did you make your sister invite us for my sake, sir? You must have known that Camilla would not enjoy such an evening.'

'Oh I was well aware of that.'

She tried to look severe.

'Then it was ill done of you to make her attend it, my lord.'

'My dear girl, I did not force her to attend, how could I?'

'She thought you wished her to be there, that you would be there yourself. However, your close friend Lord Delham was in attendance and his attentions went some way to alleviate her disappointment.'

'Delham? And how do you know that he is my close friend?'

'Because he told me so, when Lady Charlotte presented him to us: a very pleasant gentleman, made all the more interesting because his arm was in a sling. He would not tell us how it came about, of course, but Camilla is convinced it was a duel. Could it be so, sir?'

'If Lord Delham would not tell you, Miss Langridge, it is not for me to betray a confidence.'

'How infuriating!' Her eyes twinkled. 'However, I refuse to plead with you to tell me, but will ask you instead if you will be at Drury Lane tomorrow night for Mr Garrick's performance? Lord Delham tells me he is past his best, but still worth watching. Will you be there, sir?'

'That depends upon who will be attending.'

'Well, Camilla is mad for it, and Mrs Strickland has procured a box. And I believe Mr Adam Strickland is to provide an escort, so you will have no rival there for Camilla's attentions. Although I daresay her admirers will flock to the box during the interval and you would be advised to present yourself without delay.'

'I will bear that in mind, ma'am, thank you for your kind advice. Will you be there?'

She opened her eyes at him.

'But of course! How can you think I would miss such a spectacle.'

His eyes glinted down at her.

'Your innocence is misleading, Miss Langridge! Do you refer to Mr Garrick's performance, or the sight of so many men making fools of themselves over your young friend?'

Amelia laughed.

'There is some entertainment in watching grown men fall over themselves to please Camilla, but it is understandable. She *is* beautiful, is she not?'

'Beyond question.'

A tinkling bell announced Mrs Strickland emerging from the shop, quickly followed by Miss Strickland, and a footman carrying two large band-boxes. The ladies immediately fell upon the earl, assuring him that they had been enraptured by the poetry at Lady Charlotte's party, and expressing deep regret at his absence. His laughing eyes glanced over their heads towards Miss Langridge, but she had turned to study the display of hats in the window, and only the wooden-faced footman heard her mutter angrily, 'Did you expect to win a compliment? Foolish, foolish girl!'

Chapter Five

*L*ady Isabelle Pudsey let down the window of her carriage and looked out at the noisy crowds gathered in Drury Lane. She was somewhat envious of those arriving in sedan chairs, for they would at least be transported inside the theatre, while Sir Martyn would push and curse his way through the press of people, and earn for himself and his wife more jostling and sullen looks.

'Come my dear.' The coach door opened and Sir Martyn held out an imperious hand to his wife.

As they pushed their way through the noisome crowd, Isabelle pressed a posy of spring flowers to her face, praying she would not disgrace herself and be sick in the street.

'Damn you, madam, try to look a little more cheerful in my company!' Sir Martyn snarled as he pulled her into the theatre.

Lady Isabelle straightened her shoulders and tried her best to smile as they made their way to their box. Gradually the nausea abated and she could fancy herself well again, even happy, as she greeted friends and listened to her husband laughing and jesting beside her. She smoothed her apricot silk skirts, shook out her ruffles and looked about her. She saw her brother and Lord Rossleigh in a box opposite, laughing at something being said by an extremely pretty young lady who was making good use of her fan as she flirted with the gentlemen. An older lady sat beside her, whom Isabelle guessed to be her mama, dressed in a robe of rose satin trimmed with an abundance of yellow ribbons. The lady was carrying several nosegays – tokens from admirers of the young lady, she guessed, and as Lady Isabelle watched, the nosegays were handed on to another lady sitting in shadows at the back of the box. A companion, or country cousin. . . .

'And what is it that has caught your attention, madam?' Sir Martyn's voice in her ear made Isabelle jump. 'Ah, I see. Your brother, and Rossleigh.' He, raised his quizzing glass and studied the little group opposite. 'So that's Rossleigh's latest flirt. Pretty little chit, ripe for plucking! He's a fool if he ain't bedded her within the month. Who is she, do you know, Appleton?' He turned to the gentleman beside him.

'Her mama is Mrs Strickland, a widow,' came the reply. 'Kent family, I believe, some relation to young Lyddon. Just the one daughter, whom she means to marry well.'

'Then she'd better be quick about it before the girl yields to the temptations of the flesh.' He glanced down at his wife. 'You are shocked, my dear? Perhaps it surprises you to know that some women can be so free with their favours, when you find it difficult to satisfy just one man!'

Lady Isabelle turned her head away.

'Martyn, please!'

'Bah! Quit your mewling, woman!' He turned away muttering some coarse jest to Mr Appleton as the door of the box opened to admit a gentleman elegantly arrayed in a dove-grey coat with silver lacing. Sir Martyn slapped his thigh.

'Lyddon, by Gad, sir, you are in good time!'

Mr Simon Lyddon made an elegant bow to Lady Isabelle before turning to the gentlemen.

'Sir Martyn – Mr Appleton. I merely looked in to tell you that Engelman is setting up a little card party afterwards, if you would care for it.'

'Aye, and well I might, once I've seen Garrick, though I'll wager my wife will want to stay for the farce!' declared Sir Martyn jovially. 'But now, sir, a question. Is that your kinswoman yonder?'

Mr Lyddon raised his glass.

'Where – oh, there. Aye, 'tis my cousin, Mrs Strickland and her daughter.'

'Strickland eh? Never heard of the family, but perhaps the gal deserves closer attention. I shall rely upon you to present me, Lyddon!'

The gentleman gave a graceful shrug.

'As you wish, sir, but you'll find the gal hasn't a thought in her head.'

'Hah! It ain't her head that interests me,' declared Sir Martyn with a wink at Mr Appleton. Mr Lyddon turned away, his lip curling slightly, and smoothly turned the subject. He declined Sir Martyn's invitation to join them for the duration of the play, saying that tragedies were not in his line. His cool eyes rested on Lady Isabelle. The lace fichu had fallen away from her shoulder, exposing an ugly yellow and purple bruise. Aware of his gaze, Lady Isabelle quickly adjusted the lace before holding out her hand to him with such laughing assurance that his momentary frown was dispelled as he bowed over her fingers, and promised to look in again later.

If the purpose of attending the theatre was to be seen, Lady Isabelle thought they had succeeded admirably that evening, for the pit and galleries were teaming with people from all stations in life, come to see the great Mr Garrick give his performance. When Sir Martyn went off with Mr Lyddon to wait upon Mrs Strickland, Lord Delham and Earl Rossleigh made their way to Lady Isabelle's side. Lord Delham's arm was still secured in a sling, and he was obliged to spend some minutes reassuring his sister.

'It's the merest scratch, Issy, nothing to worry about. And I'll do it all again if I have to.' He sat down beside her, saying urgently, 'Only give me the word, Isabelle, and I will spirit you away from that monster.'

The lady's eyes filled with tears.

'Oh no, no, you must not say such things, Henry,' she cried. 'Martyn cannot help his temper, after all, and sometimes I am so silly . . . but you need not worry over me now, Henry, for it is all changed. I-I am carrying his child.'

Lord Delham looked into the hopeful face and closed his lips on any retort. He smiled, and patted her hand.

'Well, well, that is excellent news, my love: Pudsey will be obliged to take care of you now. Will you stay in Town, have you appointed an *accoucheur?*'

'Henry! It is far too early for anything to be decided upon, but I hope, I hope Martyn will let me go to Pudsey Court for the lying in.'

She looked up, her smile fading a little when she saw Sir Martyn had returned to the box, bringing Mr Simon Lyddon with him. Lord Delham eyed his brother-in-law with disfavour, but made a punctilious bow to Sir Martyn, who scowled at the young man.

'Come to show the world there's no rift between us, eh Delham? It's no thanks to you if tongues are wagging over your sister.'

Lord Rossleigh laid a hand on his friend's arm.

'Believe me, Sir Martyn, there is no hint of censure attached to Lady Isabelle.' The earl lifted his jewelled snuff-box and deftly flicked it open, seemingly unaware of Sir Martyn's angry glare. He took an infinitesimal pinch and dusted his fingers before continuing. 'But on a happier note, sir, I believe you were hoping to pit your mare, York Lass, against my own Lord's Folly at Epsom next month.'

Sir Martyn looked up.

'What's that? Epsom? No, my lord. I have plans far in excess of that now.'

Lord Rossleigh raised one elegant eyebrow.

'Ah. I heard a rumour that you had your eye on that pretty little mare from Petersfield's stable.'

Mr Lyddon, who had been talking with Lady Isabelle, looked up.

'What, that filly he was so keen on last season? I didn't know he had any plans to sell her.'

'We have an agreement,' said Sir Martyn curtly.

The earl had raised his quizzing glass and was idly scanning the auditorium.

'Good Gad! Is that Morcambe over there in that deplorable wig? What a fright.'

Sir Martyn visibly ground his teeth.

'The mare, Lord Rossleigh?'

'The mare? Ah yes. Petersfield's mare.' A faint smile curled his lip. 'Regret to tell you, dear sir, that she is no longer his to sell. He had a run of bad luck last night, you see.' Sir Martyn's face darkened alarmingly and a pulse throbbed visibly in his neck.

'Damn you, Rossleigh. That mare was as good as mine.'

'No no, sir. Petersfield told me he had given you first refusal *on a sale*. I acquired her as payment of a *wager*, you see. Dear me, listen to the bells: The delightful Mr Garrick must be about to entertain us. Come, Delham, we must return to our seats. Such a pity there is not time to speak to Lord Morcambe about his wig. We must do so after the performance.'

With an elegant bow to Lady Isabelle, the two gentlemen departed and as soon as they were out of the box Lord Delham exclaimed, 'Blast you, Ross. I thought Martyn would be carried off in an apoplexy. Everyone knows he's been after that mare for months.'

'Yes. Which is why I sought out Petersfield last night at White's.'

'Yes, yes, but how did you persuade him to part with her?'

'The poor man really had little choice. He was playing very deep, you know. I merely suggested a settlement.'

Lord Delham laughed.

'Good Gad man, you're a cool one: Pudsey is as mad as fire!'

'I believe he is.' The earl threw a sardonic glance at his companion. 'And much more satisfying that any duel, Henry.'

'But if you were to meet you would surely kill him,' remarked Lord Delham. 'Everyone knows you have no equal with swords or pistols!'

'Which is why Pudsey will not meet me. No, the mare is just another of those little pinpricks designed to make him itch. And all the time I grow closer to finding the secret that will ruin the man: *that* would give me greater satisfaction than merely running him through.'

His companion shook his head and placed a hand on his friend's shoulder.

'I would take care, Ross. Pudsey knows how much you hate him. Be careful he does not come up with a plan to despatch you first.'

The smile became a sneer.

'Let him try.'

'Well well, what an enjoyable evening. I think there is nothing to compare with an evening at the theatre.'

Mrs Strickland leaned back against the silk padding of the coach and sighed. The flaring torches of the houses momentarily lit the carriage as they moved off, and she frowned at her daughter.

'Pray, Camilla, why should you look so out of reason cross? You had several admirers come up to you tonight – surely that is enough for you. I was thankful that Adam was with us to attend Miss Langridge, else she would be feeling mighty neglected.'

Remembering the assiduous attentions of Mr Strickland, Amelia suppressed a shudder. The gentleman was too attentive, too eager to touch her, and all her attempts to hint him away had failed. She could only be thankful that he had gone off with his friends as soon as the play had ended and that he was not accompanying them home in the carriage. However, Miss Strickland was not at all interested in Amelia's situation. She tossed her head.

'I am sure I don't care for all those young men – so silly, most of them. Not Rossleigh, of course, but he did not stay above five minutes. But the last gentleman to come in, was he not charming? Why were you so dismissive, Mama? I was never more put out.'

'Sir Martyn Pudsey will do you no good, Camilla; he is married. It is certainly a compliment that your cousin brought him to the box, but you do not want to ruin your chances with Lord Rossleigh by encouraging his attentions.'

'Well I thought he was most kind to me. He said everything that was proper.'

'I daresay,' retorted her fond mama. 'But his wife was watching you and you must know that she is sister to Lord Delham, Rossleigh's great friend.'

Ignored in her dark corner, Miss Langridge was at liberty to review the evening. There had been ample opportunity to study human nature and she had admired Sir Martyn's tactics with the spoiled Camilla. He had been perfectly polite, but there was just enough teasing in his manner to intrigue the girl. He was older than her other suitors but his tall frame exuded power, and Amelia had heard that he was generally considered attractive. However, with so many admirers vying for her attention, Amelia did not think Camilla would dwell too long on the charms of Sir Martyn

Pudsey, especially when he could not offer her marriage.

The following morning Miss Langridge came downstairs and was immediately called upon to admire the bouquets and nosegays that had been delivered for Camilla, who was in the sunniest of moods.

'Goodness, how will I choose which one to carry to the Marchants' ball tomorrow? I am wearing my blush lustring, so Mr Avery's pinks would look very well, but Lord Rossleigh's nosegay of lilies of the valley would pin to my corsage, would it not, Mama?'

'An excellent choice, my love,' nodded Mrs Strickland. 'The earl deserves some reward for his efforts.'

Camilla inspected her flowers.

'Well,' she said smugly, 'he is my greatest admirer.'

'Certainly your richest,' put in Mr Strickland, strolling into the room. 'Lord, Camilla, are you opening a flower shop?'

'No, dear brother. You will not be so saucy to me when I am a countess.'

He grinned down at her.

'Indeed I shan't, I shall ask you to pay my tailor's bills for me!' He turned to Amelia. 'Miss Langridge, good morning to you – do you wish to go shopping this morning, or perhaps a walk in the park? I am entirely at your disposal.'

She fought down the urge to move away.

'Thank you, sir, but I shall be staying at home this morning.'

Mr Strickland was not noticeably dashed, and put forward several other schemes for her entertainment, all of which she resolutely refused, until at length the gentleman took himself off to find some breakfast. Mrs Strickland had been watching this interchange, and she moved across the room to join Miss Langridge.

'My dear, I wish you would be a little more . . . accommodating towards my poor boy.' Seeing Amelia's look of surprise she continued smoothly, 'Adam is a very agreeable young man, if only you would take the trouble to become better acquainted with him.'

Miss Langridge saw her opportunity.

'Ma'am, I do not wish to pain you, but Mr Strickland's manner towards me is too forward for my taste.'

'Too forward!' the lady laughed gently. 'I fear, dearest Amelia, that you have been far too sheltered at Langridge Court. You must not lay such store upon Adam's jokes and caresses. It is the way of the world now.'

Amelia thought of Edmund Crannock and his reserved manner. At least he did not make her feel uncomfortable.

'Dear ma'am, I pray you will speak to your son: advise him that his advances are unwelcome to me.'

Mrs Strickland laughed again and shook her head.

'I think you are becoming alarmed over nothing. Adam means no harm, my dear.'

Miss Langridge was not convinced, but it was impossible to say more. Instead she consulted her guide book and once Mr Strickland was safely out of the house and the rest of the family resting during the afternoon, she took herself off with only her maid for company to see the tombs at Westminster Abbey. While she very much enjoyed these, she decided against paying to see the dozen or so wax effigies of various sovereigns, even though her maid informed her with ghoulish delight that the effigy of Henry V had lost its head. Then it was off to the Strand to see the refurbished exterior of Northumberland House and the statue of Charles I, but to the maid's surprise Miss Langridge was not tempted to tarry in any of the fashionable shops she passed. Amelia returned several hours later, refreshed by her experience, to find that the family was preparing to go to Vauxhall gardens.

'Hurry Amelia. We are to dine early so you must change your dress quickly,' cried Mrs Strickland. 'Do you have a domino? It does not matter, you may borrow one of Camilla's.'

Miss Langridge shook her head.

'I will change my dress, ma'am, but please excuse me from going with you tonight.'

'Oh my dear: You should never have gone off jauntering, you have exhausted yourself!'

'No, I assure you I am not tired, Mrs Strickland. But I have letters to write to my family.'

'But do you not wish to see Vauxhall?'

'Very much, but it must wait, my letters cannot. Pray, madam, do not press me further. An evening at home will suit me very well, and make me appreciate all the more the Marchants' ball tomorrow evening.'

Seeing she was not to be moved, my lady tutted and shook her head, but did not press her. Mr Strickland, however, was more forthcoming. When he came down to dinner and discovered she was remaining at home, he spent the dinner hour trying to persuade her, until Amelia was obliged to bite back a sharp retort.

Once the family had departed, Amelia went to the bookroom to write her letters, but she sat for a long time with a blank sheet before her, wondering if she should ask her mama to fetch her home. She decided at length that this was too drastic a course of action. After all her mother's efforts to send her to London, she could not run away like a homesick schoolchild. With a rueful smile, Amelia wrote her letters, one to her mother describing the fashions, balls and items of gossip she knew would appeal, and a separate note to Lord Langridge, telling him of the literary figures she had met at Lady Charlotte's supper, with a detailed and highly irreverent description of Dr Johnson that she knew her grandfather would appreciate.

It was nearly midnight before she had finished and she left

her notes on the hall table before going off to bed, knowing that the family would not be back for some hours yet. Almost immediately she fell asleep, but was awoken some time later when Miss Strickland came up to her room, banging doors and chattering with her maid. Amelia tossed and turned, pulling the bedcovers over her ears in an attempt to blot out the noise and was thankful when the house grew quiet again. She was just sinking into sleep when she heard another noise that made her heart leap and thud uncomfortably. There was the sound of creaking boards and she could hear stealthy footsteps in the passage outside her room. They stopped at her door and a male voice whispered her name. Abruptly she sat up, straining to listen. The whisper came again, and a light scratching at her door. There was sufficient moonlight in the room for her to slip out of bed and see her way to the door. As she reached it she heard her name again, and recognized Mr Strickland's voice. Trembling, she put out her hand and turned the key in the lock, just as the handle began to turn. Amelia watched, horrified as he tried the door and, finding it locked, she heard his low laugh.

'Amelia, you little prude!' he hissed. 'But I am not to be dissuaded, my angel. I shall have you, never doubt it!'

She clenched her hands together to stop herself shaking, and was relieved to hear the footsteps retreating. With her heart still thudding uncomfortably she crept back to bed, pausing only to check that her window was secure. Then she lay between the covers, wide awake and waiting restlessly for the dawn.

At breakfast, Miss Langridge sought out her hostess and without giving her reasons she suggested it was time to think of bringing her visit to an end. Mrs Strickland was surprised, and mortified to think her young guest was not enjoying herself. Amelia quickly assured her that it was not the case, but since she could not bring herself to relate Mr Strickland's attempt to visit her during the night, her reasons for leaving were not convincing, and she found herself agreeing to stay another month. She returned to her room, berating herself for giving way to such persuasion. A tiny seed of doubt was beginning to grow. Amelia's sojourn with the family had shown her that their resources were limited, and she suspected her hostess would look favourably upon a match between herself and Adam Strickland. Amelia now feared that Mrs Strickland might even collude in her seduction, as a means of achieving their union. She tried to tell herself she was being fanciful, that she was not living in medieval times, but the doubt persisted. Amelia resolved to avoid being alone with Adam Strickland, and to make sure that her door was firmly locked every night.

Chapter Six

Lady Marchant's ball was a grand affair, with every public apartment opened for the evening. A slight rain had begun to fall and Mrs Strickland ordered chairs to carry them to Marchant House. They were deposited in the entrance hall, where the ladies shook out their ruffles and straightened their headdresses before making their way up the grand marble staircase to the ballroom. Entering the room between Mrs Strickland in an imposing gown of tawny silk, and Camilla wearing a new gown of rose pink damask worn over a white petticoat, caught up *à la polonaise*, Amelia felt very dull in her round gown of pale green, but her time in Town had enlarged her acquaintance and she was gratified to discover a number of gentleman eager to stand up with her. She would have been surprised to learn that some of these gentlemen truly preferred her quiet charm to Miss Strickland's dazzling beauty, and Amelia's cheerful, unassuming manners had earned her the approval of several matrons who were content to see their bachelor sons going down the dance with this elegant young woman.

Those gentlemen who were entranced by Miss Strickland were faced with the choice of standing idly by while their goddess danced with a rival or asking some other young lady to dance and many of them considered that Miss Langridge, as Miss Strickland's companion, was a good second choice.

Lord Delham was one such gentleman who, having attained one dance with Camilla, then secured Amelia's hand for a country dance and afterwards led her away in search of refreshment.

'I am sorry, Miss Langridge, that my sister is not here this evening, for I should have liked to introduce you.'

'Thank you, sir! You refer to Lady Isabelle, I think?'

'Yes.' He signalled to a passing waiter. 'I had hoped that she would be here tonight, but she sent me word that she is unwell.'

'Oh. Another time then, my lord. I shall look forward to meeting her.'

He handed her a glass of wine.

'I am sure you will like her – she is a great reader and likes all the arts, as you do, for you enjoyed Lady Charlotte's soirée, I believe.'

'I did, my lord, very much. I think I have seen your sister. Was she not at the theatre the other night?'

'Yes, she was. She—' Lord Delham broke off, grinning as he observed Lord Rossleigh approaching. 'Ross! You're dashed late, sir.'

'Servant, Miss Langridge.' The earl bowed to Amelia. 'Evening, Henry. I've been dining with Lottie, but thought I'd look in to see who is abroad this evening.'

'Aha. Well, if you have come hoping to dance with Miss Strickland, you'll be disappointed.'

The earl did not look noticeably dashed. He reached out one hand and took a glass of wine from the tray of a passing lackey, seemingly unaware that Lord Delham was scrutinizing him closely through his quizzing glass.

'Gad, sir. Is that a new waistcoat? What is it, French silk?'

'Yes.'

'Aye. Thought so, fine design, better than anything one can get in England.'

'Miss Langridge does not agree with you.'

Amelia shook her head.

'I said nothing, sir. In fact, I do agree that French silks are very fine.'

'But you look disapproving.'

'That is because I have read the petitions from our own people in Spitalfields, where livelihoods are threatened by such foreign silks.'

'Ah, but fashion transcends politics, Miss Langridge.'

She met his mocking glance with her own clear look.

'Then it should not, my lord.'

'You are not to be thinking Rossleigh uncaring, Miss Langridge,' declared Lord Delham, smiling at this exchange. 'Why, he is a great supporter of the Foundling Hospital, and a governor of the London, as well having a care for those who have lost their wits! He is forever going off to inspect some asylum or other.'

Lord Rossleigh raised his hand, saying in a pained voice, 'My dear Delham, Miss Langridge cannot be interested in such a recital.'

'On the contrary, sir, I am delighted to know that not all your energies are devoted to your waistcoats.'

'A little more could be devoted to his head, though,' said Lord Delham, looking in disgust at the earl's unpowdered locks, tied back with a simple black ribbon. 'I am surprised your man allows you out like that.'

The earl's ready grin appeared.

'O'Brien knows me too well to protest'

'Aye, well, when he's had enough of you tell him to come to me.'

Miss Langridge listened with amusement to this banter, and secretly considered the earl's gleaming brown hair looked much better than Lord Delham's pomaded wig. Lord Rossleigh wandered away shortly after, and Amelia accepted

Lord Delham's invitation to join in another country dance.

'You see, I was right!' he declared, as they took their places in the set. 'Rossleigh did come here to seek out the Strickland gal.'

Looking over his shoulder, Amelia saw Lord Rossleigh escorting Miss Strickland down to supper.

To be thus sought out by Earl Rossleigh was an honour that Miss Strickland made much of over the next few days, constantly bringing his name into the conversation with such phrases as 'When Lord Rossleigh took me in to supper. . . .' or 'Lord Rossleigh told me over supper. . . .' until the mere mention of the earl's name was enough to make Miss Langridge wince. Mr Strickland observed Amelia's reaction at dinner a few days after Lady Marchant's ball and begged his sister to stop crowing. He cast a sly glance across the table.

'I do believe Miss Langridge envies you your noble beau, Camilla.'

Miss Strickland stared at her.

'Is it true, Amelia? Lord, I would not have thought it. You poor thing. And alas for you, Adam. How can you compete with his lordship?'

Miss Langridge flushed.

'It is nothing of the sort, I assure you. Merely I have the headache this evening and any conversation makes it worse.'

'And I don't wonder at it, for this May weather has turned very close,' remarked Mrs Strickland, quite ignoring her own bickering offspring. 'Will you be well enough to come to Lady Petersfield's tonight, do you think? They say the family is quite done up, not a feather to fly with, but still the world and his wife will be there.'

'If you do not object, ma'am, I would prefer to remain here, quietly. On my own,' she added pointedly, when Mr Strickland opened his mouth to speak. This was not lost on Mrs Strickland.

'Adam, you will of course accompany us,' she said. 'Your escort will be very necessary this evening, since we are going out of Town.'

It was with relief that Miss Langridge saw the party off some hours later, and she immediately went up to her room to lie down. Although she did not have a true headache, Amelia acknowledged that she was suffering from a lowness of spirits and a vague uneasiness about remaining at Blenheim Terrace. Her appeals to her hostess to hint Mr Strickland away had had little effect, for Mrs Strickland seemed convinced that greater intimacy would result in a match between them. Also, despite sending several letters to her family, Amelia had received no word from Langridge Court and was beginning to suspect that her letters were being intercepted. Her sense of foreboding grew, and she contemplated the idea of stealing from the house and making her own way back to Somerset. She knew she did not have enough funds to travel post, but she might perhaps be able to afford a seat on the mail coach. This agreeable daydream lasted for some time, until Miss Langridge's practical nature put up objections such as how much luggage she would be able to take with her, and the objectionable gossip that would inevitably arise from her departure. She decided a more practical solution would be to write a letter to her mama, asking her to fetch her home, and to take it personally to the post office. However, even this did not wholly satisfy Miss Langridge. There was still much in London that she wanted to do and see, and the thought that she might pay another visit to the capital as Mrs Edmund Crannock was not a prospect she relished. With a sigh Amelia realized that she was, after all, a very shallow, pleasure-loving creature.

A light scratching on the door roused Miss Langridge from her reverie and a maid looked in to say that there were two visitors below wishful to see her. Miss Langridge made her way to the drawing-room where she was surprised to find Lord Delham, accompanied by a lady wrapped in a sober brown travelling cloak. Lord Delham looked up as she came in, and she saw at once that he was looking unusually serious.

'Miss Langridge, thank goodness we find you at home!'

'My lord?'

'You are surprised, and no wonder. I need your help, madam. I need a refuge for my sister.'

Amelia stared at Lord Delham, then shifted her gaze to the lady beside him. Amelia had only glimpsed Lady Isabelle at the theatre or assemblies she had attended, but then the lady had been decked out in magnificent embroidered silks, her cheeks painted and her hair piled high and heavily powdered. The face that peeped out from beneath the plain brown hood was bare of any paint and was drawn and pinched, only the luminous blue eyes showing any signs of the fabled beauty. Amelia cast another puzzled look at Lord Delham.

'Pray, won't you sit down, Lady Isabelle – my lord – and tell me how I can help you?'

'Miss Langridge, I have come to you because there is no one else I can trust. Rossleigh is out of Town, and I dare not wait for his return.'

'Pray tell me how I can help you.'

'It is a matter of some delicacy, ma'am. You can see that my sister is quite exhausted.'

'Indeed I can. She must go no further tonight.' Her mind racing, Amelia stepped forward, holding out her hand to the young woman. 'Lady Isabelle, let me take you to my room – forgive me, but I think you look ready to collapse.'

Silently Lady Isabelle allowed herself to be helped to her feet and led away. Some time later Miss Langridge returned to the drawing-room to find Lord Delham pacing the floor.

She closed the door.

'I have put Lady Isabelle in my bed, where she was close to sleep even before I left the room. I waited on her myself,' she added, noting his anxious look. 'None of the servants know her identity. However, I would like an explanation, my lord.'

'And you shall have one.'

Miss Langridge took a chair beside the fire, indicating her guest to sit down. He did so, but stared for a long time into the flames before speaking again.

'You are acquainted, Miss Langridge, with my sister's husband, Sir Martyn Pudsey?'

'Mr Lyddon brought him to the box at the theatre last week, to present him, but I think he paid scant heed to anyone except Miss Strickland.'

Lord Delham gave a short, humourless laugh.

'Mrs Strickland would do well to prevent his acquaintance with her daughter, believe me. My sister married him in the heat of passion. That was four years ago, when she was but seventeen. With no parent living, Issy was my ward. She was determined and, despite my misgivings, I accepted her choice. Lord Rossleigh was still abroad; if I had only known—'

'Known what, sir?'

He rubbed one hand across his eyes and continued, unaware of her question.

'Sir Martyn is a man of extreme moods. He has a violent temper and for some time now I have been aware that he has been venting his anger upon my sister.'

Amelia put a hand up to her cheek. 'Violently, sir?'

'Aye, dash it! Oh she does not complain, but I have seen the bruises. I have pleaded with her to leave him.' He touched the sling on his arm. 'I was even foolish enough to call him out, but all that achieved was more pain for Isabelle, and it has left me even more helpless. Then, last week, Issy told me that she was carrying his child. She was confident that the

71

violence would cease, that Pudsey would look upon her more fondly.' His good hand clenched. He said savagely, 'Could such a man ever change?' Amelia watched silently as Lord Delham fought to control his feelings, his handsome young face darkening with anger. 'I went to Petersfield's ball tonight, and soon discovered that my sister was not present, yet Pudsey was there, and in spirits, curse him. Isabelle had assured me she would be attending, because Lady Petersfield is a close friend. My hostess informed me that my sister had sent her word she was sick. I immediately went to find out for myself. At first Issy refused to see me, but I persevered and at length I gained admittance, to find her in great distress – the fiend had beaten her so badly . . . she had lost the baby.'

'Oh, poor lady!' exclaimed Miss Langridge.

'Aye, but at least she was now willing to leave him. However, she is in such dread of the man that she dared not bring even her maid. I could not persuade her to approach any of her friends nor will she take refuge with me, so afraid is she that he will find her and force her to return to him. Rossleigh is the only one I would trust to protect her — the only one that Isabelle herself would turn to. But he is out of Town. If she were well, I would even now take her with me to my house in Leicestershire, and if Pudsey dared to follow I would put a bullet through his black heart.'

'My lord, until you yourself are fully restored to health you must not consider confronting Sir Martyn,' protested Miss Langridge. 'Your sister is safe here, for a few days at least, and I shall pass her off as my school friend, Miss — er — Weston.'

Impulsively he took her hand, and kissed it.

'Madam. You are very good.'

'Thank you, my lord. I am happy to help you, but . . . our acquaintance is so slight, why did you come to me?'

'Rossleigh,' he said simply.

Miss Langridge stared.

'But, I hardly know the earl.'

It was Lord Delham's turn to look surprised.

'However that may be, Miss Langridge, he speaks very highly of you. He tells me you are a sensible woman, and I know he greatly admires your practical spirit. Also, Isabelle tells me that she does not know Mrs Strickland or her family, so there is little likelihood that she will be recognized here.'

Thinking of the pale, frightened child asleep in her bed, Amelia thought it impossible that anyone would connect her with the vivacious, fashionable Lady Isabelle Pudsey.

'What will you do now, Lord Delham?'

'Rossleigh will be back in Town tomorrow. I will consult him, then we will spirit Issy away. Until then, no one must know where to find her.' He looked up. 'Miss Langridge, I am sorry to impose on you, and upon such short acquaintance. Believe me I should not have done so if I could see any other way.'

Amelia nodded. 'We will manage it, my lord. Your sister will be plain Miss Weston. Be assured that I will look after her.'

Lord Delham took her hand again. 'Thank you, ma'am. Will you be at the Russells' fire work party tomorrow night?'

'Mrs Strickland is planning to go, and I am invited. However, in the circumstances I had thought to cry off. . . .'

'No, no, be there. We can talk again without attracting attention.'

'Very well, sir. You will see me there.'

After Lord Delham had left, Miss Langridge sat for a long time beside the fire, pondering this latest turn of events. The arrival of Lady Isabelle meant that she must postpone any plans to leave Town, but at least with 'Miss Weston' sharing her room she need not fear a night-time visit from Mr Adam Strickland. Yet the aspect of the matter that occupied most of

Amelia's thoughts was Lord Rossleigh's role: what could he have said to Lord Delham to make him believe she could be trusted in such a delicate situation? She recalled Lord Delham's words – a sensible woman. Well, there appeared to be few enough of those in Town. The thought that she would forego all her good sense for a brief, heady flirtation with the earl was quickly suppressed. It would be folly for her to think that such a connoisseur of women as Earl Rossleigh would ever spare her a second glance.

Chapter Seven

Lord Rossleigh's second trip to Home End was accomplished in brilliant sunshine. He arrived at Weir Cottage to find the door standing open and a sandy-haired lady in a dimity gown and snowy apron stirring a cooking pot suspended over the fire. She looked up as the earl's shadow fell across the doorway, frowning. The earl stepped inside and gave her his most charming smile.

'Mrs Wilmot, I have no doubt – Mr Graby's sister.'

Slightly reassured by his words and polite tone, the woman relaxed a little.

'That's right, sir, but who might you be?'

'I called upon Mr Graby some weeks ago and promised to return. Is he here?'

She jerked her head towards the back room.

'He's in there, sir. He fell on his hip last Sunday and since then he's not left his bed. But I've no doubt he'll see you, heaven knows there's little enough to occupy him here.'

Lord Rossleigh went through to the back room where he found the old man in a trestle bed, propped up against a bank of greying pillows. At the sight of his visitor the old man's eyes widened.

'So you've come back.'

'As I said I would. How are you?'

'Well enough to write, thank God!' The old man's sharp

eyes rested on the earl. 'You'll pay me for my story? I promise you I know enough to take Pudsey to the gallows.'

'When he is convicted you shall have your money.'

'And you'll give me protection?'

'You will be required as a witness. You will have the protection of the courts. But before I make your statement known to anyone I will arrange for you to be moved to the safety of my estates.'

'And a pension for life?'

'As we agreed.'

The old man stared at him.

'And you won't move against Sir Martyn until I am safe?'

'You have my word on that.'

The old man nodded. 'I'll write to you as soon as I am up and about again. Come, then, if you have brought the paper, ink and pens let us get on with the business!'

'Why the urgency?'

The old man gasped as he pulled himself up in the bed.

'Your visit brought it all back to me, damn you! I thought I had put it behind me, but I find I can't rest with it on my conscience. Then when I fell on my hip it seemed like a warning . . . not that I'm a religious man, never was, but there's some things Sir Martyn did that I didn't hold with, and never shall. Give me the paper; I'll write it now and my sister shall sign it.'

The daylight was almost gone when Lord Rossleigh finally left Weir Cottage. Mrs Wilmot followed him outside and turned to lock the door behind her. Then she stood for a moment looking up at the earl.

'I can't say I know just what I signed for Nathan, but he knows I won't be a party to any wrongdoing and he says it's all within the law. Is that so, my lord?'

The earl patted his pocket, feeling the crisp sheets of paper safely stored there.

'Yes, mistress. Your brother was servant to an evil man and his information will help to seal his fate.'

'Aye, I was afraid for a while the evil might have rubbed off on Nathan, but if it's as you say, my lord.' She continued to study his face for a long moment then, as if satisfied, with what she saw, she nodded and turned to make her way home.

Lord Rossleigh walked back to the Bell Inn where he had left his horse. He declined Master Taylor's offer of supper and a bed for the night, confident that the rising moon would provide sufficient light for the homeward journey. As he rode away, he was unaware of the weasel-faced man watching him from the shadows.

Chapter Eight

*A*round midnight Miss Langridge went up to her room, where Lady Isabelle was still sleeping soundly. By drawing the curtains around the bed Amelia was able to light several candles and unpack the lady's portmanteau without disturbing her guest. When she heard Mrs Strickland return she made her way downstairs, to inform her that they had another guest. She was relieved that Miss Strickland had gone straight to her room, but she found Mrs Strickland and her son in the drawing-room and, praying that the servants had not recognized Lord Delham, she launched into her story, which was received with no little surprise.

'She is staying here?'

'Why yes, ma'am. I hope you do not object. Miss Weston was due to travel to the West Country with her brother on the morning mail when she was taken ill this evening, and having no other acquaintance in Town, Mr Weston brought her to me.' She gave Mrs Strickland her sunniest smile. 'I have tucked her up snugly in my bed.'

'Did you say she is ill?' cried Mrs Strickland, recoiling. 'Is she . . . contagious?'

'No, no. Miss Weston is merely suffering from exhaustion. I thought you would not object to her sharing my room? She is such a dear friend, and I could not turn her away.'

'Of course not.'

Mr Strickland, who had been listening to this exchange, raised his head.

'How long is she likely to stay?'

'Oh, no more than a few days. As soon as she has regained her strength she will be continuing her journey with her brother. He has taken a room with a male friend,' added Amelia, in an attempt to head off more difficult questions, 'but *that* of course would be quite unsuitable for a gently bred young lady.'

'Of course,' murmured Mrs Strickland.

Scowling, Mr Strickland bade the ladies goodnight and set off for his rooms in Half Moon Street. Once he had gone, Amelia bade her bemused hostess a hasty goodnight before she could pose any further questions.

The following morning Miss Langridge explained the subterfuge to Lady Isabelle who was sitting up in bed, sipping hot chocolate. My lady listened attentively and even managed a wan smile.

'Miss Langridge, I am so grateful to you for helping me in this. My – my husband will be sure to search for me, and I have no doubt that he will have Delham watched, also. No one will dream that I have come to you because we have never even spoken before.'

'And you are very sure that you are not known to Mrs Strickland?'

'Well, we may have attended the same party, but that is all. . . .'

'You need not look so uncomfortable, ma'am,' said Miss Langridge, with a rueful smile. 'I am well aware that Mrs Strickland is not accepted in the highest circles. She receives invitations to the larger parties, but cannot attain the intimacy with the Ton that she craves.'

Lady Pudsey coloured. 'I am sorry – I did not wish to offend you.' She sighed. 'I doubt anyone would recognize me now, for I have never before ventured out in Town without my powder. My brother insisted that I should bring only my plainest gown with me, to avoid attention.'

Amelia took her hand and squeezed it.

'And I will do my best to make sure Mrs Strickland thinks you quite unworthy of comment, *Miss Weston.*'

When Amelia joined the family later in the morning she was prepared to be quizzed on her visitor. Camilla, learning that 'Miss Weston' was an impecunious school friend with little money and no connections, soon lost interest.

'I suppose it means you will not be coming to the park with us,' she said pettishly. 'And after Adam has hired a gig for us, too.'

Miss Langridge excused herself, but assured Mrs Strickland that she would be accompanying them to Russell House that evening.

'Miss Weston is too exhausted to leave her room today, and she does not object to my leaving her for a few hours tonight. Which reminds me.' She summoned her sweetest smile. 'The key is gone missing from my door, ma'am. I have questioned the housekeeper, who said she will arrange for another to be made for me, but in the meantime she suggested I might borrow yours?'

'Well, I—'

Amelia smiled at her.

'Miss Weston, you see, has a very nervous disposition and is used to locking her door.'

Mrs Strickland pouted, shrugged, and finally agreed to find a key for Miss Langridge's door before dinner.

Amelia spent most of the day with Lady Isabelle and was heartened to observe her swift recovery. When she set off for Russell House that evening she carried with her reassuring messages for Lord Delham. Mr Strickland was to escort them and joined them for dinner at Blenheim Terrace. Amelia responded coolly to his overtures, but when the carriage arrived to take them to the party, he seated himself next to her. She felt his leg pressing against hers as he bent his head to whisper in her ear.

'This makes up a little for your absence all afternoon.'

He was rewarded with a frosty glance and she turned away from him, noting with dismay that Mrs Strickland was nodding and beaming at her son from across the carriage. The drive to Russell House, situated on the western fringe of Kensington village, was accomplished swiftly but by the time the carriage pulled up on the sweeping drive before Lady Russell's Palladian mansion, Amelia was heartily sick of Mr Strickland's attentions. He lost no opportunity to squeeze her arm or touch her knee as he pointed out some landmark or building that he thought she might find of interest. When they moved into the crowded entrance hall her irritation was so great that she used the ensuing confusion and bustle to inform Mr Strickland that no power on earth would make her dance with him that evening. With relief she watched him lounge off to the card-room.

Mrs Strickland observed her son's departure with some dismay.

'Oh dear, where is Adam going now? I had hoped he would lead you out for the minuet, Amelia. You must save him another dance, my dear.'

'No, ma'am. I have already told him that I will not dance with him,' retorted Amelia, her patience exhausted. 'I find him altogether too forward.'

Mrs Strickland smiled at her. 'Well well, young men can be a little hasty when their interest is aroused.' She stopped and turned to Amelia, taking her hands and squeezing them. 'You could go a long way before you found a better husband, my dear.'

Miss Langridge felt her cheeks grow hot.

'Mrs Strickland—'

'Hush now. I know you are too modest to admit to any such thoughts, but give it a little time, and I am sure we will be able to persuade you to look upon his suit favourably.'

She patted Amelia's arm and turned to ascend the sweeping staircase. Seething with frustration, Miss Langridge accompanied her, but once they reached the ballroom she excused herself and went over to the open windows leading out to the terrace, hoping that the evening air would cool both her cheeks and her indignation. The sun had gone down, but there was still enough light to show the well-tended gardens, and at the edge of the park the timber scaffolding erected for the firework display.

'I thought I saw you come out here.'

'Lord Rossleigh.'

With the orchestra striking up for the first dance, all the other guests had moved to the ballroom. They were alone.

'I understand that you have an — ah — an old friend staying with you?'

Miss Langridge was still too angry at Mr Strickland's behaviour to smile, or to pretend to misunderstand him.

'Thanks to you, I believe.'

'I'm sorry. I had no idea Delham would involve you in this. I had much rather he had not'

His apology disarmed her.

'My anger this evening is not aimed at you, my lord. Indeed, I am only too glad to help. You have already spoken to Lord Delham?'

'Yes. The difficulty now is to find somewhere safe for the lady out of Town. Pudsey will certainly search for her on Delham's estates and mine. He is unscrupulous, and will stop at nothing to find her. I would like to believe it is because he has some affection for Lady Isabelle, but I cannot. It is merely his dislike of being thwarted that will make him search for her.'

'I have been thinking the matter over, and if I might suggest,' Miss Langridge began tentatively. 'My old governess resides near Bath. She lives retired, but is quite genteel, and if – if the lady would consent to go there . . . it would not be in the first style of elegance, of course, but Miss Templecombe lives very comfortably. The lady would be safely out of her husband's way until you can make some other, more permanent arrangement.'

He bent his searching gaze upon her.

'Do you think this governess of yours would take her in?'

'Oh yes, and cosset her shamefully! She is a most delightful creature and once the situation is explained she could be relied upon to look after the lady.'

He took her hand and raised it to his lips.

'Miss Langridge you are a genius, I salute you! How soon can you write to this paragon?'

'Why, I will do so tomorrow.' She hesitated. 'Could one of your people take the letter? I-I believe Mrs Strickland is – obstructing my correspondence.'

His brows snapped together.

'Of course, I will take the letter myself. But what is this—'

'Hush! Here is Lord Delham come to find us! I will walk out to Bond Street tomorrow morning. If you can contrive to be there, I will pass the letter to you.' She turned to hold out her hand to Lord Delham. 'Good evening, my lord. Forgive me if I leave you – Lord Rossleigh will explain everything, and it is better if we are not seen together.' She slipped into the ballroom and was soon lost amongst the chattering crowd.

'So?' enquired Lord Delham. 'Is it all arranged?'

Lord Rossleigh quickly informed him what had been agreed.

'A perfect solution! Miss Langridge is an angel!'

'I agree with you, Henry, but I wish you had not embroiled her in this affair. It could be dangerous.'

'I know, Ross, but I could think of no one else to help me. We must get Issy out of London as soon as possible. You will take the letter to Bath yourself?'

'Yes, I will leave tomorrow.'

'You are a good friend to me, sir!'

The earl's crooked grin appeared.

'You know I will do anything to serve Pudsey an ill-turn, and there seems a certain justice in this one!' He looked up when a figure appeared on the terrace, his smile widening as he saw Sir Martyn coming towards them. 'Ah, my dear Pudsey,' he murmured. 'Lost something, sir?'

Sir Martyn's face darkened.

'Nothing that cannot be retrieved. I know how to look after my own, Rossleigh.' He glanced towards Lord Delham, who made as elegant a bow as was possible with one arm resting in a sling.

'Good evening, Sir Martyn. So where is m'sister tonight?'

'I'll wager you know well enough where she is, sir!'

'Do I, though?' mused Delham.

'She left my house with you last night, damn you. Where is she?'

It was Lord Delham's turn to sneer. 'We Delhams also know how to look after our own!'

Sir Martyn took a step forwards, but in an instant the earl was between them.

'Now now, my dear Pudsey. A man with one arm bound up is surely not an equal match for you. I, on the other hand, am only too ready to give you satisfaction.'

A tense silence covered the terrace. Sir Martyn, breathing heavily, stared into the earl's icy blue eyes and read mockery in their depths. For a full minute they stood thus, then Sir Martyn stepped back.

'You go too far, Rossleigh,' he ground out. 'I have warned you not to meddle in my affairs.'

The earl's fingers played with the ribbon of his quizzing glass while a mocking smile lifted the corners of his mouth.

'Your warnings are to little effect, it seems.'

Sir Martyn was about to reply but a sudden burst of laughter heralded the appearance of a merry group of guests on the terrace. He hesitated, then his black scowl was replaced with a cold smile that did nothing to dispel the menace from his eyes. He bowed, turned on his heel and walked off. Lord Delham exhaled.

'Good Gad, Ross. He was within a whisker of calling you out.'

'Surpringly, I am pleased he did not,' murmured the earl. 'Our friend has a dark secret, and once I have proved that and exposed him, he will be destroyed more fully than with any bullet.'

Chapter Nine

To Miss Langridge, watching from the side of the room, it seemed that Lord Rossleigh had given himself up wholly to the pleasures of the evening. He danced twice with Miss Strickland, then led out a very dashing matron with an abundance of red curls before disappearing into the card-room. She herself was not short of partners, and thought perhaps it was the excitement of arranging Lady Isabelle's flight that had left the rest of the evening feeling sadly flat. She danced once with Lord Delham, and as they moved around the floor her eyes fell upon Mrs Strickland and her daughter deep in conversation with a tall gentleman in puce satin.

'You frown, Miss Langridge. Is it because of my dancing?'

Lord Delham's teasing voice recalled her to her duty.

'No, sir, not at all.' She lowered her voice. 'I am a little uneasy to see Sir Martyn talking with Mrs Strickland.'

Lord Delham glanced across the room.

'Judging by Miss Strickland's demeanour he is paying her a host of compliments. He has the look of a cat surveying its next meal.'

'Poor Camilla then. I know I should not be anxious, for your sister's disappearance is not yet generally known and even if it were, plain little Miss Weston bears no resemblance to the magnificent Lady Isabelle. And Mrs Strickland is unlikely to mention the existence of my penniless school friend to anyone.'

Lord Delham grinned at her.

'Very true, madam.' The music ended and he made her an elegant bow. 'I would offer to take you down to supper, but we must not give anyone cause to think us anything more than the merest acquaintance. I will leave you now, but believe me, I am deeply indebted to you.'

As midnight approached all the doors and windows leading to the terrace were thrown open and everyone moved out into the gardens to watch the fireworks. The guests spilled down the shallow steps into the gardens, spreading out to obtain the best place to view the forthcoming display set up on the far side of the park. Amelia followed Mrs Strickland out into the darkness, but as she did so the fringe of her wrap became ensnared on one of the bushes growing in a tub on the terrace. She was obliged to stop and disentangle it, but she was hampered by the fan and reticule hanging from one wrist, and the need to use one hand to hold her wrap about her.

'Allow me, madam.'

Lord Rossleigh was beside her, and his lean fingers began to tease the fringe free of the woody stems. He was standing very close to Amelia, and he said, without looking up from his task, 'What did you mean, Miss Langridge, when you said that Mrs Strickland might be intercepting your letters?'

She felt the colour staining her cheeks.

'Perhaps I am being fanciful. Mrs Strickland is eager for me to prolong my visit here: I fear she does not want me to ask my grandfather to fetch me home.' She stopped, aware that her story sounded foolishly weak, as if she was merely homesick, but even so she could not bring herself to voice her fears about Adam Strickland.

Having freed her wrap, the earl regarded her with a sceptical light in his eyes, but at that moment Miss Strickland came up to them.

'Lord Rossleigh, are you engaged? Mama says she is sure you will know the very best place to stand to enjoy the fireworks.'

Amelia murmured her thanks and moved away, but not before she had seen the earl offer his arm to Camilla.

'Indeed I do, Miss Strickland. In fact, I know the perfect place, removed from the crush, but with an uninterrupted view of the display. . . .' He walked off with the lady on his arm, smiling blandly at Sir Martyn as they reached the steps.

Miss Langridge observed Sir Martyn's venomous look and she shivered, praying he would never find out that she was hiding his wife from him.

There was a sudden rushing sound as the first wave of fireworks sailed upwards. The crowd gasped and applauded as a many-coloured fountain spilled out over the night sky, followed by a second wave of rockets that burst noisily overhead.

'Ah there you are.' She felt a hand on her arm. Adam Strickland smiled down at her. 'Come over here, Miss Langridge, I think you will find the view superior.'

He guided her to the side of the terrace, away from the lights of the ballroom. The noise of the fireworks was increasing, and Amelia firmly removed her arm from Mr Strickland's grasp and stepped away from him. Then she forgot her companion and watched enraptured as the sky exploded into crimson, blue and white stars. Rockets screeched overhead and flares drenched the whole scene in a rosy glow until at length they reached the climax of the display, a naval battle with two large ships depicted in a blaze of fiery colour and a lifelike cannonade that brought cheers from the crowd.

As darkness descended once more over the gardens Amelia joined in the enthusiastic applause.

'Oh what an ingenious display!' she cried. 'I have never seen its like before.'

'Have you not? They are quite commonplace in Town these days.' Mr Strickland took her arm again and patted her fingers. 'If you like I will take you to Ranelagh the next time there are fireworks.'

This was said so much in the manner of an elderly relative offering a child a treat that Miss Langridge could not help smiling as she murmured her thanks. His restrained behaviour persuaded her to dance the next two dances with him, but although he behaved with perfect propriety, she could not be sorry when Mrs Strickland announced that their coach awaited them. She felt desperately tired, and leaned back in her corner while Mrs Strickland and her daughter chattered away about the evening. For Camilla it seemed that the spectacular fireworks were eclipsed by the triumph of adding another name to her list of admirers.

'Did you see, Mama, how attentive Sir Martyn was to me?'

Camilla's careless words roused Amelia from her sleepy state. Mrs Strickland gave a little laugh.

'He was entranced by you, my love.'

Miss Langridge felt compelled to speak.

'You know of course that he is married.'

'Oh pho! What do I care for that.' declared Camilla, tossing her head. 'I mean to be a countess, but it does no harm to show Rossleigh that I am admired by other men.'

'Take care, Camilla. I do not think Sir Martyn should be trifled with – nor, for that matter should Lord Rossleigh.'

Mr Strickland stirred in his corner.

'Stap me, Miss Langridge. You're a fine one to talk about trifling, when you play fast and loose with my heart.'

'Mr Strickland I have never given you any encouragement to hope—' Miss Langridge began indignantly, but found Mrs Strickland's hand upon her arm.

'Hush, my dear. Can you not see that dear Adam is funning?'

'Madam, I really must protest!'

'I know, Miss Langridge, I know you think he goes too far, but consider, the evening has been such a success, the wine was flowing so freely, it is not to be wondered that my son should be in high spirits. You should look upon his attentions as a compliment.'

Realizing she would never make them understand her position, Amelia closed her lips upon an angry retort and sank back into her corner. She had hoped that they would drop Mr Strickland at Half Moon Street, but he announced his intention of escorting them all to Blenheim Terrace. When they reached the house Amelia went inside, determined to retire immediately. However, as the butler bore down upon his mistress, Mr Strickland gripped Amelia's arm and hissed that they must talk.

Amelia was tired and angry. She wanted nothing so much as her bed, but she decided that instead of an unseemly struggle in the hall in front of the servants she would allow Mr Strickland to say his piece and then make it plain to him that his suit was hopeless. She therefore led the way to the morning-room.

While a footman lit the candles in the room Amelia took off her wrap and laid it over a chair. Then she stood beside the empty hearth, her hands loosely clasped before her and fixed Mr Strickland with a cool, appraising gaze. His speech was much as she had imagined. He began by telling her that from their first meeting he had been struck by her beauty, charm and elegance, then he progressed to his admiration of her modesty and finally declared his undying love for her. Amelia listened in silence. Faced with such an unmoved auditor, Mr Strickland's confidence began to falter and when he launched upon a tangled and somewhat incomprehensible description of his prospects and estates, Miss Langridge put up her hand.

'Thank you, sir. You have said quite enough, I think. Since I first set foot in this house you have subjected me to attentions that have been as unpleasant as they have been unwelcome. I have never given you the slightest encouragement, indeed I have made it as plain to you as I could without resorting to incivility that I did not wish to receive your attentions, yet you have continued to pursue me – yes sir, pursue me. I came to London without any thought of marriage and if I *was* looking for a husband, which I am not, I can assure you it would not be yourself!'

Mr Strickland listened to this plain speech in growing amazement. Spoiled from birth, and encouraged to think that his florid good looks were universally pleasing, he found it impossible to believe that any young lady could find him unattractive. Now he smiled.

'Your nature is too reserved, Miss Langridge. When you know me better—'

'Sir, I have no wish to know you better.'

Mr Strickland's smile turned into a leer.

'Nonsense, my dear. I know you are like a little bird that has been captive all its life. The cage is open but you are afraid to taste freedom.'

'I assure you, sir, I have all the freedom I require.' She stepped back as he moved towards her, but he was too quick for her. He caught her arm and swung her towards him, pinning her against his chest.

'Don't fight me,' he muttered, trying to cover her face with kisses. 'Let yourself enjoy this.'

He had clamped her against him with his left arm while his right hand forced her chin up and she felt his hot, brandy-fumed breath on her face before his lips locked on to hers.

At that moment the door opened.

'I think I saw them come in here. . . .' Mrs Strickland's voice trailed off as she stepped into the room and saw Miss Langridge in the arms of her son. At the sound of his mother's voice Mr Strickland loosened his grip on Amelia, whose eyes widened in horror as she looked towards the door. There, standing behind Mrs Strickland, was Edmund Crannock.

Chapter Ten

*A*melia pushed Mr Strickland away. Her cheeks were flushed with embarrassment but it was anger that sparkled in her eyes. Mr Strickland, equally flushed, muttered an excuse and lounged out of the room. Mrs Strickland watched him go and tried to find her voice.

'Well,' she said at last. 'Well, Amelia – here is Mr Crannock come all the way from Bath to bring you news of your family.'

Miss Langridge summoned a smile and stepped forward, holding our her hand.

'Edmund. What – what a pleasant surprise. But what are you doing here so late?'

Obviously shocked by the scene he had witnessed Mr Crannock struggled for an answer.

'I arrived in London but an hour ago, and having secured a room at the George I thought I would walk round and see where you were staying – the lights were still burning and I decided to leave a message for you. However, as I was giving instruction to the footman my lady's coach arrived at the door and I decided to wait and speak to you, to tell you immediately how your mother and grandfather go on.'

'How kind,' murmured Mrs Strickland, relieved that at least she was not expected to house another friend of Miss Langridge. 'Shall we return to the drawing-room? Andrews has set out refreshment there for us.'

As they crossed the hall Mr Crannock fell into step beside Miss Langridge.

'Really Amelia!' he hissed in a furious whisper. 'What are you about to be indulging in such behaviour? And who was that man?'

'Mrs Strickland's son – and I was not indulging in anything!' she hissed back. 'If you think I encouraged him to kiss me, you are glaringly abroad, Edmund!'

Mr Crannock looked pained.

'Such cant terms sit ill upon a lady's lips, madam.'

Biting back a retort, Amelia stalked ahead of him into the drawing-room.

Mrs Strickland, still looking bemused, invited Mr Crannock to sit down.

'So fortunate we were back in time to meet you, sir.'

'Yes indeed, ma'am. It was my intention merely to leave my letters, but when your carriage arrived, I could not resist the opportunity to see Miss Langridge.'

Mrs Strickland looked a little taken aback by such devotion, and merely nodded silently.

'You may think it a little forward of me, at such a late hour,' he continued, smiling. 'but perhaps Miss Langridge has not explained to you that I am a near neighbour of Lord Langridge, and regarded very much as one of the family.' This was said with such emphasis that Amelia felt her indignation growing again.

Mr Crannock drew a fat packet of letters from his pocket and handed them to Amelia.

'Your mama knows how it is when young ladies are busy with parties and balls every night, it is impossible to find time to write.' Although this confirmed her suspicions that her letters had not reached Langridge Court, Amelia still flushed at his reproachful tone. 'When your mama knew of my intention to come to Town she gave me these for you —

she was so pleased that she could write to you without having to cross her lines! You will of course read them at your leisure, but I am pleased to be able to inform you, Miss Langridge, that I left both your mother and grandfather in good health. However you must know, my dear Amelia, that your absence is sorely felt at Langridge Court.'

Amelia's spirits were far too agitated for her to give more than a murmured reply but Mrs Strickland said all that was proper and Mr Crannock, apologizing again for the lateness of the hour, finally rose to take his leave. He bowed low over Amelia's hand.

'I shall call again in the morning, when we can talk further.'

'I am so sorry, Edmund, but I am going out in the morning. I have a commission in Bond Street.'

He blinked.

'Shopping, Amelia? Can that not wait?'

'I am afraid not. I have to collect a bonnet.'

Amelia realized how petty this sounded, but she was too cross to try to mollify Mr Crannock. However, he was not so easily dismissed.

'Then I shall escort you. Tell me when you wish me to call for you.'

Having agreed a time, the gentleman finally took his leave and Amelia could at last retire. She was accompanied to her door by her hostess.

'Mr Crannock is very devoted to you, Miss Langridge. He has made such efforts to see you,' remarked Mrs Strickland. 'He hinted to me that there is an understanding between your families?'

'The gentleman sometimes takes too much upon himself!' retorted Amelia, still seething over the events of the evening.

Miss Strickland relaxed a little.

'So there is nothing settled between you? How wise, my

dear. It is best for young ladies to go about the world a little before making such a decision.'

Too late Amelia realized she had missed her opportunity, but although she found Mr Strickland's clumsy attentions repugnant, she was even more reluctant to encourage Edmund Crannock's complaisant assumption that she would marry him.

A restless night did not provide a solution to her problems, but she refused to dwell on them and prepared for her trip to Bond Street in a mood of determined cheerfulness, spurred on by Lady Isabelle's enthusiasm for the suggestion that she should live with Miss Langridge's old governess for a short time.

'It is so good of you to take such trouble when you hardly know me,' murmured my lady, clasping Amelia's hand.

Miss Langridge smiled warmly at her.

'I know of you, my lady, and I hope, when we are safely out of this tangle, that we may become good friends!'

Mr Crannock appeared promptly to escort Miss Langridge to Bond Street and she talked happily to him about Langridge Court, encouraging him to tell her all that had happened since she had left. Mr Crannock's recital of his daily visits to the Court, his search for a new gardener for his own grounds and his detailed plans to introduce a new breed of dairy cattle would have dampened the sunniest of spirits, but Miss Langridge paid scant heed to his words, for as they approached Bond Street she was looking out for Lord Rossleigh.

'Is this the milliner?' asked Mr Crannock, as they made their way along the crowded thoroughfare.

'I beg your pardon?'

He pointed towards a shop window.

'Is this the shop you require — you are collecting a bonnet, are you not?'

'Oh, oh of course. Yes.'

Requesting Mr Crannock to wait for her outside, Amelia disappeared into the shop, returning a few minutes later to say brightly, 'The silly woman has mistaken the day. It is not ready.'

'Really, Amelia, I had thought you above such fripperies as a new bonnet!'

'Did you? I confess I myself did not know how exciting shopping could be until I came to Town!'

She ignored his silent disapproval, for she had spotted her quarry.

Lord Rossleigh was coming towards them, his sister on his arm and two liveried footmen walking behind them, laden with parcels. It was only natural that they should stop and Miss Langridge presented her escort to the earl and his sister.

'Mr Crannock is our neighbour in Somerset,' she explained, trying to ignore the mocking gleam in the earl's blue eyes.

'Good day to you, sir. Do you make a long stay in Town?'

Mr Crannock shrugged and cast a speaking look at Amelia.

'That depends upon circumstance, my lord. I have several commissions to undertake, and there is a lecture at the Royal Society that I should like to attend. . . .'

Lady Charlotte expressed her interest in the sciences, and while she engaged Mr Crannock's attention, Miss Langridge grasped her opportunity. She tried to open her reticule while holding her parasol and gloves, and everything slipped from her fingers. She stooped to collect up her belongings and the earl did the same, so that in the confusion she was able to slip him the note she had written to Miss Templecombe, her ex-governess.

'A suitor if ever I saw one,' murmured the earl, wickedly. 'And you tell me you are a novice at dalliance, Miss

Langridge. Yet you are so accomplished at it!'

Amelia threw him a scorching look but dare not speak because Mr Crannock was already preparing to move on.

'I am going out of Town for a few days,' said the earl, handing Amelia her parasol. 'In fact, I leave this afternoon. However I hope to return in time for my sister's masque on Friday. I trust you will be there, Miss Langridge?'

'And you must come too, Mr Crannock, if you are still in Town,' put in Lady Charlotte with a friendly smile.

'Your ladyship is too good, but I did not come prepared for parties.'

'A masque would be a little too frivolous for you, would it not, Edmund?' murmured Amelia.

He frowned at her.

'Oh come now, sir. Such a party is not to be missed!' laughed the earl. 'There will be dancing, cards and the prettiest women in Town all gathered for your entertainment!'

Mr Crannock could not disguise his repugnance.

'Thank you, sir, but I avoid such indulgence. I prefer an evening of rational debate, with learned men distinguished in the arts and sciences.'

The earl's eyes gleamed, but it was Lady Charlotte who replied.

'Indeed sir, so do I. However, one must have a little levity at times, you know, or we should become such very dull creatures.'

Mr Crannock would not be drawn and they parted with Lady Charlotte promising to send him an invitation and saying that she relied upon Miss Langridge to persuade him.

'It seems to me,' pronounced the gentleman as they made their way back to Blenheim Terrace. 'It appears to me that your time in London is spent in an excess of pleasure and — and indulgence.'

'Edmund, if you use that word once more I will box your

ears!' retorted Miss Langridge. 'Mrs Strickland and her daughter enjoy all these parties and routs, and it would be churlish of me not to attend, but I have also visited the sights of the capital, and attended a literary supper, which was very stimulating. . . .'

'And does Mr Strickland accompany you on these outings?'

'Occasionally, but his company is not something I enjoy.'

He stopped.

'Are you telling me you did not encourage his advances last night?'

With an effort she curbed her temper.

'I have already told you so, Edmund. I find his attentions most distasteful.'

He laid a hand over hers where it rested on his arm.

'Only say the word, Amelia, and give me the right to protect you from all such importunities.'

'Edmund – thank you, I know you mean well, but I am sorry, it is not possible.'

For a moment she thought he would argue, but with a sigh he accepted her words and they strolled on.

'I see what it is,' he said. 'You cannot be expected to think of such important matters while you are living in this whirl of entertainment. Very well, I will let you enjoy your time in London, Amelia, as long as you realize that this is not your world. It is all as much a charade as – as Lady Charlotte's masked ball. At some point you must come back to Langridge Court and face your responsibilities.'

Miss Langridge felt her spirits dip: if facing her responsibilities meant marrying Edmund she found the prospect depressing indeed.

When Miss Langridge set off for Bond Street with Mr Crannock, she left Lady Isabelle sipping at her hot chocolate. She had lost her fear of living in a strange house, for she had been readily accepted as Miss Weston and was confident that Sir Martyn would never think of looking for her in this household, for although she thought highly of Amelia, it was plain to Isabelle that Mrs Strickland and her daughter moved on the edge of society, attending the larger balls and public entertainments but denied access to those intimate circles in which Sir Martyn and his wife moved freely. It was only a few days since she had fled her husband's house, but already Lady Isabelle was looking much better. Her skin still showed the bruises Sir Martyn had inflicted, and her spirits ached for the baby she had lost, but away from her husband and the constant threat of violence she felt a weight lifted from her mind. To while away the morning, she took the tambour frame and silks that Amelia had loaned her and went to sit in the morning-room. She dare not go out of doors, but Isabelle felt strangely liberated in this house where she was not subject to constant scrutiny and no one criticized her every move. She was just thinking how pleasant it would be always to live like this when the door opened and Mr Simon Lyddon walked in.

'Oh!' The tambour frame slid from her fingers.

'I beg your pardon, ma'am – I understood the family was still abed.' He stooped to pick up the embroidery. 'You must be Miss Langridge's friend. We have not been introduced. . . .' He trailed off as he looked into the pale face with its large, anxious blue eyes. 'L-Lady *Isabelle?*'

She put her hands to her white cheeks.

'Oh heavens I am undone!'

He continued to stare at her.

'No, no – that is.' Mr Lyddon took a few hasty steps about the room, trying to collect his thoughts. 'Sir Martyn said – I thought—' He broke off, then turned to frown at her. 'You have not gone out of Town, then. There have been rumours, of course, but – is it true, you have left him?'

She hung her head. Two large tears ran over her cheeks and dripped into her lap. He came to sit beside her, handing her his own handkerchief.

'Dry your eyes, madam. I cannot bear to see you cry.'

'Th-thank you.' She looked up at him. 'Please, tell no one I am here! If M-Martyn learns of it. . . .' She shuddered.

'You need have no fear, Lady Isabelle, I will not betray you.'

'I fear he will kill me if he finds me.'

'Trust me, my lady, I would do nothing in the world to hurt you. But how do you come to be here? I did not know you were acquainted with the family.'

'I am not, but my brother knows Miss Langridge and she agreed to help me. I had nowhere else to hide until Delham can find me safe lodging out of Town.'

'Good God what a pickle! And do you hope for a reconciliation?'

She shook her head, wiping away her tears.

'N-no. S-Sir Martyn will not change, and his temper – I am in fear of my life, sir.'

'I can believe it, for I have seen his anger for myself.' He fell silent, a brooding frown on his brow, but presently he shook himself out of his reverie. 'You must be wondering why I am here.'

'I had forgotten that Mrs Strickland is your cousin.'

'Aye, and I have been used to treat this house very much as my own, which is why I walked in on you unannounced. Have you breakfasted? No? Well, neither have I, so I shall instruct Andrews to bring us some ratafia and a plate of macaroons. What do you say?'

She gave a watery chuckle.

'That is not a true breakfast, sir.'

'I know, but I think it will put some heart in you.' He moved to the door and sent a footman running to do his bidding before returning to apply himself to the task of cheering the lady. He succeeded so well that Isabelle was disappointed when he announced that he must leave her.

'Those creaking boards above us tell me the family is stirring and do you know, I have lost all interest in seeing them today. I shall leave word with Andrews; he can be very discreet, you know. May I call upon you again, "Miss Weston"?'

'Oh, yes, if you please. But – you will tell no one where I am?'

'No, trust me. I shall forget I ever saw you here.' With a final bow he kissed her hands and went away. Isabelle ran to the window to watch him stride off down the street then returned to the sofa, reliving the past half-hour. She glanced in wonder at the dainty plate that had held the macaroons – if it were not for the crumbs and the dregs of wine in their glasses she would have thought she had dreamed the whole.

Chapter Eleven

*M*iss Langridge returned at noon and was informed by the butler that Miss Weston was still in the morning-room.

'Well,' she said, smiling at Isabelle. 'My letter to Miss Templecombe is now with Lord Rossleigh, who is setting off to see her today.'

'Thank you. Who was the gentleman who escorted you to the door?'

'Mr Crannock, a neighbour of mine from Somerset. I told him you were not well enough to receive visitors – I hope you do not mind, but I was glad to be able to send him away, a little of his company is more than sufficient. I fear he means to return tonight to dine with us, for he has persuaded Mrs Strickland to issue a half-hearted invitation. Do you think you could bear to eat with us, or shall I tell our hostess that you will keep to your room?'

Lady Isabelle was in fact so well recovered that not only was 'Miss Weston' able to come down for dinner, but she even accompanied the ladies to the drawing-room while Mr Strickland and Mr Crannock enjoyed their brandy. The gentlemen did not tarry long, for although neither admitted to it, they regarded themselves as rivals for Miss Langridge's affections and struggled to maintain their civility to one another.

Mrs Strickland rarely spent an evening at home, and for her part Amelia would have preferred to have no guests. Warned of 'Miss Weston's' precarious health, Mr Crannock addressed only the most innocuous remarks to her and spent the rest of his time vying with Mr Strickland for Amelia's attention. Camilla found the evening unutterably tedious, for she was used to being the centre of attention and she was about to take herself off to bed when Mr Lyddon was announced.

Miss Langridge felt her heart sink. She glanced towards Isabelle, but she appeared unaware of any danger. Mr Lyddon entered the room and Amelia held her breath as Mrs Strickland presented him to Miss Weston. She was surprised at the cool way he was received, but apart from a faint, rosy flush on her cheek, Isabelle betrayed no sign that she reccgnized the gentleman, and even allowed him to sit beside her and engage her in conversation. Amelia remarked on this when they were retired. She had dismissed her maid and was herself brushing out Isabelle's fair curls.

'I admit I was in a fever of apprehension lest Mr Lyddon should recognize you.'

Lady Isabelle met her eyes in the mirror and smiled.

'No, were you worried? He gave no sign of knowing me.' She began to rearrange the bottles on the dressing-table. 'He – he is a very pleasant gentleman, is he not?'

'Oh, exceedingly good company. I thought he enlivened the evening considerably. However I believe he is an inveterate gambler, with not a feather to fly with.'

'But – but very kind, and I think that is more important in a gentleman than fortune, do you not agree?'

Miss Langridge returned a non-committal answer and bustled her charge off to bed, praying that Lord Delham would be able to spirit his sister out of Town before any further complications could arise.

When Lord Rossleigh's note arrived for Miss Langridge two days later, she quickly made its contents known to Lady Isabelle.

'Lord Rossleigh has returned. He has seen Miss Templecombe, who is only too delighted to help us: I knew it would be so.'

'Oh. When do we depart?'

'I am to take you to the Golden Lion this afternoon and your brother will take you from there to Midford. You need not fret, Isabelle. Miss Templecombe has the kindest of hearts and she will take very great care of you.'

My lady hugged her.

'I do not doubt it, if you say so, Amelia. I am so grateful for all you have done for me, I cannot begin to tell you—'

'Then don't,' laughed Amelia. 'Pack up your things and I will tell Mrs Strickland that you have a seat booked on the mail today. She will not think it strange that I want to see you on your way.'

'But will she not think it odd, my leaving so suddenly?'

A mischievous twinkle sparkled in Amelia's grey eyes.

'Undoubtedly, but she will be even more thankful to have you gone!'

Explaining Miss Weston's departure proved easier than Amelia had expected. Camilla had awoken complaining of a sore throat and Mrs Strickland was too distracted with preparing gargles and possets for her daughter to spare more than a passing thought for her guest. She paid little heed to Amelia's explanation of tickets and letters and said merely that Amelia should do as she thought best. Thus at three o'clock Miss Langridge and her heavily veiled companion took a hackney coach to the Golden Lion, where they were shown into a private parlour. Lord Delham was waiting for them and Lady Isabelle ran to him, to be ruthlessly hugged.

'Well, little sister, you look so much better than when I last saw you! And you see, I have left off my sling, so that I have two arms to embrace you.' He held out a hand to Amelia. 'Miss Langridge, I am in your debt. You have taken excellent care of her.'

'It was nothing, sir. And you are now fully recovered?'

'Pretty much. There is a little stiffness, but that will go.' He turned as the door opened to admit Lord Rossleigh, who came in shaking the rain from his hat.

'The carriage is ready, Henry – Lady Isabelle, Miss Langridge. I am sorry to bring you out in such inclement weather.'

'We took a carriage sir, so the rain did not affect us, although it may hamper your journey into Somerset, Lord Delham,' replied Miss Langridge. 'The road to Bath is liable to flooding.'

'Then the sooner we get on our way the better,' declared my lord, picking up Isabelle's portmanteau and moving towards the door.

'Goodbye, Miss Langridge, thank you again for all you have done! Ross.' He turned to grip the earl's hand. 'I shall be back in a couple of days, as soon as I have made sure Issy is safe.'

'God speed, Henry. You will find I have put two good men on the box, both armed.' He saw Lady Isabelle's look of dismay and added, 'A precaution, merely. You will be travelling in a plain carriage, in case Pudsey is watching the roads, out of Town.' He took Lady Isabelle's hand and kissed her fingers, giving them a reassuring squeeze before he let them go. 'Be brave, my lady. We will untangle this coil, never fear.'

Lord Rossleigh waited until Lady Isabelle and her brother had passed out of the room then he shut the door.

'It is best if we wait here until they are gone. We must do nothing to attract undue attention to that carriage.'

Amelia looked out of the latticed window as the coach-and-four pulled out of the yard.

'What will Sir Martyn do if he finds her?'

'Kill her,' Came the blunt reply.

She stared at him.

'Surely sir, you do not think—'

'I do. He is quite ruthless.'

'So there can be no going back.'

'No.'

'Poor Lady Isabelle.'

'At least she is out of his power. She at least has a chance to recover.' He paused and she thought he would say more, but when he turned he merely said, 'My carriage is outside, madam. Will you allow me to take you up?'

Looking at the rain sheeting down in the yard Miss Langridge felt unequal to the task of finding a chair to take her home, and she gratefully accepted.

'Your directions were very clear, Miss Langridge,' remarked the earl, as the steps were put up. 'I found Miss Templecombe quite easily. And you were correct, she is a most sensible woman. I am most happy to commend Lady Isabelle to her care.'

'I am relieved that she is leaving Town at last.'

'Has it been a worry for you? I am sorry.'

'No, no, forgive me, I did not mean to complain. "Miss Weston" was a most unexacting house guest, and I shall miss her company.'

'Will you be at my sister's masque tomorrow?'

'Yes. I know it is you we must thank for the invitation.'

He turned to look at her.

'You would rather not go?'

'On the contrary, I am looking forward to it.'

'But? Come, Miss Langridge, I can tell from your voice that something is troubling you.'

She smiled. 'Am I that transparent?'

'To me, yes! Tell me.'

'I cannot make up my mind if you mean it as a reward to me for helping Lady Isabelle – in which case it is quite unnecessary. Or . . . or if it is to pursue your flirtation with Camilla.'

She met his frowning eyes and coloured slightly. 'If it is the latter you will say it is none of my business!'

'I should not be so impolite.'

'But you would think it.'

The frown lifted.

'Gad, Miss Langridge, a man must be allowed his thoughts!'

She was not satisfied, and bit her lip. He reached for her hand.

'Miss Langridge, the invitation is not due to any sense of gratitude, nor is it designed to flatter Miss Strickland. I want you to be there. Will that suffice?'

She blushed rosily.

'But we – we are not of your world, my lord.'

'You are gently born, that is sufficient.' He paused. 'Do you tell me Mrs Strickland would prefer to stay away?'

'Of course not. It is her ambition to attend such select gatherings.'

She realized he was still holding her hand, but could not bring herself to pull away. The carriage came to a stand outside Mrs Strickland's house. The earl's grip on her fingers tightened.

'Miss Langridge, pray give me the pleasure of your company at my sister's house tomorrow night.' He paused. 'Or perhaps you are afraid I will frighten off your admirers.'

She laughed. 'Sir, you may do that with my blessing!'

Chapter Twelve

*A*t the time that Lord Delham drove out of London with his sister, a much more plebeian coach arrived in the capital and was depositing its passengers at a small hostelry in Lawrence Lane. The driver mopped his brow with a large spotted handkerchief and watched the passengers alight. His uninterested gaze passed over the impecunious cleric in his worn black frock-coat and the harassed mother with two crying children, whom she cuffed soundly before leading them off through the teeming streets. His eyes lingered for a moment on the plump and pretty maid in her snowy mob-cap with her calico skirts caught up to display a neat ankle, but he gave no more than a cursory glance to the soberly dressed lady in a black bonnet and shawl who alighted last from his carriage. The woman gripped her basket tightly and looked up and down the street, then turned to ask directions from one of the stable lads before setting off westwards with a purposeful step.

At length she reached a charming terrace of large town houses, their stone frontages gleaming in the afternoon sunshine. She walked along slowly, looking up at each one until she reached her goal. Then with a firm tread she mounted the steps and rapped loudly at the knocker. A liveried footman opened the door, his brows raised disdainfully at the sight of the diminutive figure before him.

'I would like to see Lord Rossleigh.'

The footman's eyebrows rose even higher.

'There is a door round the back for those looking for work. The housekeeper will see you there.'

'I am not looking for work, and I have no wish to see the housekeeper. Pray direct me to Lord Rossleigh.'

The footman was somewhat surprised by this forthright speech, but he did not move to open the door any wider.

'His lordship is not at home to visitors.'

The woman put up her chin.

'He will see me.'

Lord Rossleigh was at his desk when his butler entered and stood hesitating in the study doorway.

'Well, Foye, what is it?'

'There is a – a female downstairs, my lord, who demands to speak with you.'

'A female, Foye? Can't you deal with it?'

'I regret, sir, that she refuses to tell me anything, except that she wishes to speak to you.' He coughed delicately. 'I would hazard that she is a respectable woman, my lord, and possibly from the country. Gave her name as Wilmot.'

My lord put down his pen.

'Send her up, Foye.' He blotted his letter and tidied his desk until the butler announced his visitor, then with a courteous smile he walked forward to greet her, saying pleasantly, 'Mrs Wilmot, this is a pleasure, madam. Will you sit down?'

She nodded slightly and took a seat beside the desk, putting her basket carefully on the floor beside her.

'Not a pleasure, my lord, but I wanted to see you.'

The earl looked at her intently, waiting for her to continue.

'Nathan is dead,' she said baldly.

'I am very sorry – was it the result of his fall?'

She fixed her eyes on him in a painfully direct gaze.

'No, my lord. His cottage was burned to the ground the very night that you came to see him.'

Lord Rossleigh stared at her, the smile quite gone from his face.

'Tell me,' he said.

Mrs Wilmot hesitated.

'I remembered you telling Nathan that you would be wantin' him as a witness, so I reckoned that you wouldn't want him dead.'

'I did not. His deposition is useful, but a witness would have made our case much stronger.' He pulled up a chair and sat facing her, leaning forward with his elbows resting on his knees and his long fingers clasped together. He said again, 'Tell me what happened.'

'You will recall that we left the cottage together, my lord, and I locked up securely behind us. I know that you went back to the inn and fetched your horse, for I asked Sam Taylor and he told me you had not stayed. It was in the middle of the night when Sam's young lad comes a-knocking on the farmhouse door, yelling that Weir Cottage is afire, so Mr Wilmot and me we runs down to the village, but by that time the place is well alight.' She paused to pull out a crisp white handkerchief and proceeded to wipe her eyes. 'When . . . when we could eventually get inside we f-found Nathan's remains, still in his bed.' She looked up at him, her face tight with anger. 'My lord, you know there was no candle burning when we left Nathan. He was settled to sleep for the night, and I had covered the fire.'

'You are saying this was not an accident?'

'Sam says there was a stranger in the tap-room that night, a thin-faced little man who came in during the evening and skulked in the corner all night, keeping an eye on the window that looks out on to the yard. He left soon after you rode away.'

110

'Oh? And do you think Master Taylor would recognize the man again?'

She nodded.

'Sam's an innkeeper, my lord, and prides himself on his ability to recognize faces.'

'Catling,' murmured the earl. 'I may have inadvertently led Pudsey's spies to the cottage.' He bowed his head. 'I am sorry.'

'And so am I, sir. But I have the comfort of knowing that Nathan was doing the right thing in the end. God will have mercy on him for that.'

A silence hung over the room for a few moments, then Lord Rossleigh turned to his guest.

'Mrs Wilmot, I still have your brother's statement, and I promised to reward him. Perhaps you would like—'

She put up her hand.

'No, no, Wilmot and I have sufficient, and to take money in such circumstances would sit ill with me. No.' she picked up her basket. 'What I want is justice for my brother, my lord, and I hope that this might help you to get it.'

Reaching into the basket, she pulled out a leather-bound notebook.

Chapter Thirteen

'Well, what do you think?' Camilla tripped into Miss Langridge's bedroom and spread her skirts, turning this way and that to let the light catch on the tiny seed pearls sewn over her gown. She was wearing a leaf-green open robe over a yellow petticoat, and a stomacher heavily embroidered with spring flowers. Camilla's dusky curls were caught up in a yellow ribbon and from her fingers dangled a green leafy mask.

'You look charming, Camilla. What are you, a wood nymph?'

Miss Strickland stood before the mirror and critically studied her reflection.

'No, I am Flora, goddess of flowers and the spring.' She spread her fan, displaying the fine chicken-skin painted with a woodland scene. 'Look, I have a matching fan, and flowers embroidered on my slippers, too.'

'Delightful.'

'It is well enough, I suppose. I wanted to be Venus, only Mama said it would not be seemly, and she does not wish to offend Lady Charlotte.' Camilla cast a brief glance at Miss Langridge, who was fastening a sapphire domino over her gown.

'Did you not wish to dress as a character?'

'I have been too distracted to think of it.' Amelia picked up her loo mask. 'This will do very well for me. Come, let us find your mama.'

'She is already downstairs, with Adam.'

Miss Langridge's spirits dipped a little but she was not surprised that Mr Strickland was to join them; such a prestigious invitation was not to be ignored and Mrs Strickland would have insisted upon her son's attendance.

Although the hoops and panniers of former days were now only worn at Court, the ladies' gowns filled the carriage and even threatened to billow out of the windows. However, the journey to Redcliffe House was not long and the party was soon making its way up the marble staircase to the glittering assembly rooms where Miss Strickland could not contain a gasp of delight at the colourful assembly. Everyone was masked and either wearing an enveloping domino or dressed in fantastical costume. Lady Redcliffe herself greeted them dressed in a sumptuous gown of black velvet sewn with precious stones and quantities of gold thread.

'Persephone,' she explained to Amelia, her eyes twinkling. 'A little joke of Redcliffe's. He dislikes the time we spend in Town so much that he likens it to Persephone's months in Hades. The rubies and amber are clustered together to resemble pomegranate seeds.'

'It is very elegant ma'am.'

My lady laughed.

'You are being polite, my dear! Ross says it is vulgarly ostentatious, which is true, but such fun!' She swept away to greet another guest and Amelia followed Mrs Strickland on towards the ballroom. A large orchestra played from a raised dais at one end of the room and the dancers swirled about beneath the huge chandeliers that glittered from the high ceiling. She was surprised to see Sir Martyn Pudsey was present and felt a moment's panic as he came purposefully towards her. However, after bowing to Mrs Strickland he turned with a smile to Camilla to beg the honour of a dance.

'Too late, Pudsey!' drawled a mocking voice at his shoulder. Lord Rossleigh stepped passed him, magnificent in black and gold, and took Camilla's hand, giving her his most charming smile.

'Our dance, I think, Miss Strickland.'

Camilla gazed up at him, open-mouthed. She was aware of a tension in the air that she did not understand, but she was thrilled to be sought by two such elegant gentlemen. With her hand firmly on Lord Rossleigh's arm she gave Sir Martyn a shy, apologetic smile.

'As you see, sir, I am promised. But I am free for the Allemande, later.'

'Dear, dear, Pudsey,' murmured the earl. 'All your ladies are deserting you, it seems.'

Miss Langridge held her breath, watching Sir Martyn's hand clench on the hilt of his dress sword. Without a word he made a perfunctory bow and turned on his heel.

Mr Strickland had persuaded Amelia to partner him for the first dance, and as he was escorting her back to Mrs Strickland she saw Mr Crannock making his way towards them. A purple domino hung about his shoulders and he had exchanged his usual brown bag-wig for a white-powdered Ramillies that was more in keeping with the occasion but accentuated his ruddy cheeks. Having thanked Mr Strickland, Amelia turned to greet him.

'Edmund, so you decided to come, after all.'

He bowed to her, then acknowledged Mr Strickland with barely a nod, his stance reminding Amelia very much of a belligerent bulldog. She tried to be charitable.

'I am so pleased to see you – you are even wearing a mask;

well done, sir.'

'Not well done at all, merely following custom,' he said heavily. 'And not at all necessary: such wisps of black silk do little to disguise an identity.'

Amelia helped herself to a glass of champagne from a passing waiter as she summoned up a smile.

'That is too bad of you sir,' declared Mr Strickland. 'Surely you appreciate how fine a lady's eyes appear when seen through the slits of her mask.' He smiled archly at Amelia, then, feeling he had acquitted himself very well, he went off to find another dancing partner. Mr Crannock glared at his departing figure.

'I had thought you above this sort of thing, Amelia.'

'Above what sort of thing?' she enquired, her eyes glittering dangerously. 'Enjoying myself? I hope I shall never be above that!'

'No of course not, that is not what I meant. Let us dance.'

'Only if you promise to smile, sir.'

With an effort Mr Crannock managed a slight upward curve to his lips as he led his partner out. The carnival atmosphere was infectious and the champagne made Amelia feel a little light-headed. She tried to joke with her partner, but Mr Crannock was not a natural dancer and he was obliged to concentrate upon his steps rather than engage her in idle banter. After one dance it was a relief to find Mr Strickland waiting to lead her out again: at least he knew how to entertain a lady on the dance floor. However, she soon found his lover-like attentions almost as distasteful as Mr Crannock's reticence and resigned herself to the fact that she was exceedingly difficult to please. The activity and numerous candles made the rooms very hot, and a continuous stream of footmen passed through the crowds carrying trays filled with glasses of wine, champagne and lemonade to refresh the dancers. Amelia soon lost count of the champagne glasses she picked up, but by midnight everything around her seemed noisier and more colourful. She had refused to stand up with either Mr Crannock or Mr Strickland for a third dance, and when they began to argue over who was to fetch her a glass of lemonade she bade them both go away, saying pettishly that she was better without them. Standing alone at the side of the room, however, she began to regret her rash words.

'Your suitors appear to have deserted you, Miss Langridge.'

She raised her chin, steadily meeting Lord Rossleigh's quizzical glance.

'No, my lord. I sent them away. Their bickering was making me cross.'

'Then will you dance with me?'

'Only if you promise not to pay me fulsome compliments, nor lecture me on the immorality of such occasions as these.'

He took her hand.

'Is that what your suitors were doing?'

'Yes,' she said bitterly. 'Edmund even had the effrontery to tell me that ladies of breeding abhor such occasions as these, and that I should reflect upon the moral dangers of wearing a mask.'

His lips twitched.

'I have no doubt that is what you were doing when I came up to you.'

'No,' she admitted. 'I was thinking that I quite *like* being told that my eyes are shining like stars tonight.'

'And your lips are like red cherries, ripe for plucking?'

'Yes!' she said defiantly.

He shook his head at her, his eyes glinting. 'Fie, Miss Langridge, I thought you said you wanted no fulsome compliments.'

'I did say that, but – oh I don't know *what* I want, except that I do not want to be sensible this evening!'

He laughed as the dance separated them and they said no more, but when the music ended, instead of taking her back to Mrs Strickland he led her in the opposite direction, towards the long windows that opened out on to a wide balcony. These had been opened to allow a little air into the crowded room, and they stepped out on to the balcony. As they moved further into the darkness, the sounds of the shouts and laughter from the ballroom became muted. Above them the moonless sky was dotted with diamond-bright stars. The earl led her to the end of the balcony where he turned her to face him. Exhilarated by the heady mix of dancing and champagne, she gave a contented sigh and smiled up at him.

'Do you know, your eyes really do put the stars to shame, Miss Langridge. And your lips, so soft.' He ran a finger over her cheek, his thumb just brushing her bottom lip.

Amelia was aware of a sudden stillness in the air. Her heart was thudding so hard that she found it difficult to breathe. The laughter had fled from the earl's eyes and he looked down at her now with a quite different expression, one that sent a tingle of fear trembling down her spine. She felt quite faint, achingly aware of how close they were. His head slowly came down until his lips were brushing hers with exquisite tenderness.

Another few seconds and she knew she would lose all control. Her arms longed to hold him, she wanted to abandon every precept of modesty, but even as she felt her willpower slipping away, discordant voices broke into her consciousness. The earl was also aware of them. He raised his head and looked back towards the open window. Two figures had stepped out on to the balcony, and Amelia heard Mr Strickland's angry voice.

'And I say you jostled me, sir. It was deliberate, and I demand satisfaction!'

'Devil take you sir, I never touched you,' retorted an equally angry Mr Crannock.

'Oho, afraid to face me, is that it?'

So engrossed were they in their quarrel that they were not aware of anyone else on the balcony. At the first sound of their voices Lord Rossleigh had moved to shield the lady from view, but she stepped past him, staring in amazement to see the two gentlemen standing breast to breast, each one in a towering rage. As Amelia watched, Mr Crannock took one pace back, stripped off his gloves and struck his opponent across the cheek.

'Edmund!' Amelia ran forward and grasped his arm. 'Edmund. What are you doing?'

He shook her off.

'Go away, Amelia. This is no place for you.'

Aghast, she stared at Mr Strickland. His jaw was clenched and a muscle worked angrily in his cheek.

'Mr Strickland – you must see that Edmund is not quite sober.'

He ignored her.

'Name your friends, sir.'

This practicality seemed to deflate Mr Crannock slightly.

'I – that is—'

Mr Strickland was already calling to his cousin, who had strolled out to see what was happening.

'Simon – you will act for me?'

Mr Lyddon took in the situation quickly and bowed.

'Aye, Adam, if you wish it.'

Mr Strickland turned back to his opponent.

'Well, sir?'

'You must know, sir,' Edmund began stiffly, 'that I have only recently arrived in Town, I have no acquaintance—'

'Perhaps I may be of assistance.' Lord Rossleigh stepped up, his eyes gleaming with unholy amusement. He bowed to

Mr Crannock. 'I would be happy to act for you, sir.'

'No!' cried Amelia. Again she laid a hand on Edmund's arm. 'Please – consider what you do.'

He looked down at her, frowning.

'Madam, do, pray, go away,' he said coldly. 'Do you wish to give rise to even more gossip?'

She fell back as if he had slapped her. She looked from Edmund's stern face to the earl's mocking smile, and angry tears began to prick her eyelids. With a huff of exasperation she pushed through the crowd that was gathering in the window, surprised to find the orchestra was still playing, and couples still dancing, unaware of the drama taking place only a few yards away. She noted idly that Camilla was standing beside Sir Martyn, their heads very close together as they talked. It seemed quite unimportant, nothing mattered now except the quarrel taking place on the balcony.

Some ten minutes later Mr Crannock appeared. He was very white, and made straight for the door. Amelia ran to intercept him.

'Edmund, Edmund, what has happened? Tell me.'

He glanced at her for a moment as if he did not recognize her, then he firmly moved her aside.

'Excuse me, Amelia. I am leaving.'

'But why – Edmund, why did you quarrel with Adam Strickland?'

'You should know that very well, madam.'

'No, how can I? Edmund, please tell me!'

He shook off her hand.

'Out of my way, Miss Langridge. I must go home if I am to be at my best in the morning.'

Horrified she watched him walk away, feeling that she had somehow wandered into a nightmare. She looked in vain for Lord Rossleigh or Mr Strickland as the party continued around her. The unmasking passed with little merriment for her: she wanted merely to go home. At last she spotted Simon Lyddon and made her way towards him.

'Sir – tell me, what was the cause of the quarrel between your cousin and Mr Crannock? Pray do not tell me it is not my concern,' she added, as he hesitated. 'I was there when the challenge was issued.'

'Then you will know, ma'am. Strickland holds that Crannock jostled him.'

'But that is so trivial!'

'Enough for a man to demand satisfaction, Miss Langridge.'

She shook her head, disbelieving.

'This is dreadful! Can you not stop them – as Mr Strickland's second are you not bound to seek out a settlement?'

Mr Lyddon looked uncomfortable.

'Well yes, we will discuss it, of course, but these things are best left to run their course.' He gave her what she thought was meant to be a reassuring smile and moved on, leaving Amelia more anxious than ever. She sought out Lord Rossleigh. He listened to her impassioned arguments that he should find a way to settle the matter peacefully, then shook his head.

'They don't want that, Miss Langridge. And in truth, I have my own reasons for wanting them to continue: they came out on to the terrace and interrupted a very enjoyable episode.'

She ignored his flippancy.

'But one of them could be killed.'

He considered the matter.

'Oh I shouldn't think so. Devilish hard to hit someone you know, even for a skilled marksman.'

Her eyes filled with tears.

'How can you be so heartless. Don't you care?'

'No, why should I?' His look softened and he touched her

cheek with one finger, saying softly, 'Don't worry, my sweet. They will meet in the morning, their heads will ache like the very devil and they will both fire wide. We shall then retire to a local inn for a good breakfast, honour having been satisfied.'

She turned away from him.

'I will never understand gentlemen.'

The earl gave her a crooked smile.

'I have been saying the same of your sex ever since I was a schoolboy. Go home, Miss Langridge, and try to sleep. Everything will be well, I promise you.'

Amelia was unable to follow his advice but when she came downstairs the following morning after a sleepless night, she was informed that Mr Strickland was in the breakfast-room. She found him helping himself to a cup of coffee.

'Good morning, Miss Langridge. Promised Mama and Camilla that I would escort them to the Strand this morning, although I am perhaps a little early.'

She looked at him closely. He was certainly pale, but perfectly composed.

'You are not hurt – you have fought the – the duel?'

A look of distaste crossed his features.

'How unfortunate that you should be present at that little scrap last night. This is not a matter for ladies.'

'But you have met with Mr Crannock?'

'Yes. And as you see, I am not injured.'

'And Mr Crannock?'

'Not a scratch.'

She sat down at the table and dropped her head in her hands.

'Oh thank God.'

Mr Strickland lowered his cup.

'I would be interested to know if your concern is for

Crannock, or for me, ma'am.'

'Neither!' she declared, jumping to her feet. 'I think I would be pleased if all men were to annihilate one another.'

And with that, she ran out of the room.

Chapter Fourteen

With her maid in attendance, Miss Langridge embarked on a brisk walk in St James's Park in an attempt to calm the violent agitation that besieged her emotions. She was relieved that neither gentleman had come to any harm, but she knew that underlying this was a dissatisfaction, a depression that Lord Rossleigh had failed her. She had turned to him for help, and he had refused her. Berating herself as a fool for thinking he would help her, she resolved to put the matter from her mind and spent the remainder of her walk thinking of very violent but highly implausible ways of exacting revenge upon the earl.

At about the same time Lord Delham was calling at Rossleigh House. He was shown into the dining-room, where the earl was enjoying a solitary breakfast.

'Good morning, Henry.' The earl waved at him from across the table. 'Have you come to join me? Shall I have a place set for you?'

'No, I thank you. I have already broken my fast, but I will help myself to a glass of small beer, if I may.'

'So, when did you get back to Town?' asked Lord Rossleigh, dismissing the footman.

'Yesterday evening. I left Bath in the morning and called in upon Isabelle on my way back to London. She is secure enough. Her hostess is a sensible woman and will keep her safe. I'm pretty sure we were not followed, so there is no reason for Pudsey to search that area. Issy was fretting because of Midford's proximity to Keynsham but I assured her it was far enough removed for her to be easy.'

'Keynsham? Why should that worry her? Pudsey has no property there.'

Lord Delham shrugged.

'Issy says Pudsey's agent has mentioned the place, and she has seen Sir Martyn address correspondence to someone in that area.'

Lord Rossleigh frowned.

'Keynsham. I know of no connection there, but it might be worth investigation.'

'Still looking for the scandal to ruin Pudsey?' murmured Lord Delham, smiling faintly.

Lord Rossleigh returned his look.

'More than that, Henry. I am now sure I can achieve his downfall. But to return to your sister, Midford and Keynsham are on opposites sides of Bath, Isabelle should be safe enough for the present.' He grinned. 'Word is out, you know, that she has run away. Pudsey is furious but putting on a brave face.'

Lord Delham nodded.

'I returned to find that his man has been to my rooms, asking questions. My people won't talk, of course, but even so I've been careful to keep my sister's direction from them. However that wasn't the talk at the clubs last night. I called in at Brooks's to see if you were there, since I was much too late for your sister's party. But I learned that you had gone straight home – to prepare for a duel.'

'Oh, who told you that?'

'Bumped into Adderbrook, he was at y'sister's masque when the quarrel broke out – Strickland and some country squire, I believe.' Lord Delham looked enquiringly at his friend. 'Well, Ross, are you going to tell me the whole?'

'I have no doubt Adderbrook has already done so.'

'No, how could he? He didn't know Strickland's opponent, although from his description I'd wager it was Miss Langridge's friend.'

'Aye, it was Crannock, but I'd rather you did not link Miss Langridge's name with this affair.'

'Happy to oblige you, my friend, but Adderbrook tells me she was there when the quarrel broke out, so there's already a whisper. Tell me the whole.'

'I happened to be on hand when Strickland issued the challenge. Crannock, of course, is new to Town, and had no one to stand for him, so I – er – offered to do so.'

'The devil you did!'

The earl's eyes gleamed.

'Gave me the chance to use my new duelling pistols.'

'Good God, sir, you're a cool one. You showed me those pops, do you remember? We tried 'em out. They're damnably accurate! Anyone killed?'

'No. Not even winged.'

'Hah! Deloped, did they? Well, Miss Langridge will be relieved – I suppose the quarrel was over her? Oh don't look down your nose at me like that, Ross. You know I wouldn't say anything outside this room, but it's been plain to me that the pair of 'em have been vying for her attentions. I'm dashed glad of it, too. She goes everywhere in the shadow of the Strickland chit, and damme if she don't deserve some attention herself! Mrs Strickland is not good Ton, Ross. She's a mushroom trying to climb into society. Dashed if I don't think Miss Langridge would do better to find herself another chaperon.'

'Well said, Henry, if a little inconsistent. I thought you had an interest in the – ah – Strickland chit yourself.'

His young friend flushed. 'Well, I don't say I wasn't dazzled at first, and she knows how to be agreeable, but there's precious little behind that pretty face.'

'Can't condemn Mrs Strickland for trying to make a good match for her daughter.'

'Not at all, but it won't be me.' He grinned. 'I've a notion she's set her cap at you, Ross. Best be careful, old friend, or she'll have you leg-shackled before the year is out.'

'Thank you for your concern, Henry. By the by, has Mrs S sent you an invitation to her little party on Friday?'

'Lord yes, but I doubt I shall go. Apart from the beauty's youthful admirers it's bound to be full of cits and toadies. Not our sort of thing at all, very dull work.'

The earl pushed away his plate.

'Delham, you disappoint me. I have already decided I shall go, and I shall expect you to accompany me!'

Lord Delham was not alone in his opinion of the forthcoming event. Mr Crannock had already told Amelia that he would not be attending. It was the morning of the party and he found Amelia helping her hostess with the rearranging of the furniture, ready for the evening's entertainment.

'I cannot give you long, Edmund,' she said, accompanying him into the morning-room. 'Mrs Strickland has charged me with preparing the rooms, and there is still much to do. She is determined to have dancing, and so the drawing-room has to be cleared.'

'I merely came to explain why I will be absent,' he told her. 'I am already engaged to attend a lecture at the Royal Society, but I cannot say I am sorry to be missing an evening of such fruitless frivolity and excess.'

Amelia wanted to tell him that she would far rather go with him to the lecture, but loyalty to her hostess kept her silent.

'I cannot see,' went on Mr Crannock, warming to his theme, 'that since coming to Town you have spent one evening in useful endeavour.'

'And if I were at home, Edmund, would my time be better spent?' she replied, trying to keep her temper. 'My evenings there consist of sewing with Mama or playing backgammon with my grandfather.'

'Now you are being foolish, Amelia! You know that at home you have your books and your painting.'

'As I have here.'

He ignored this.

'There is also the garden, which you keep so admirably.'

She could not help smiling at that.

'Edmund, now it is you who are being foolish. You know I do little more than discuss the grounds with my gardener. His is the inspiration for the garden.'

'My dear Amelia you are too modest. I know your judgement in such matters is excellent. In fact,' he added, allowing himself a little smile, 'I am hoping I can persuade you to help me with a little project for my own grounds – I plan to dig up the west lawn and have a water garden there next year!'

The look that accompanied these words implied a high treat for Amelia, and she replied with suitable gravity.

'Thank you, Edmund. I am honoured by your faith in my ability.'

He nodded, and took her hand as he said goodbye, adding with an arch smile, 'There, I have given you something pleasant to think of tonight, have I not?'

Miss Langridge hoped that she would have something more exciting than gardens to occupy her thoughts that evening, but a glance at Mrs Strickland's guest list made her doubt it. A number of young gentleman had been invited at Camilla's instigation, and several matrons with daughters of marriageable age were bringing their charges in the knowledge that even an acknowledged beauty could not dance with more than one man at a time. A further glance at the list made Amelia acutely aware that Mrs Strickland's attempts to draw the *beau monde* to her house had not been successful. She could imagine the graceful little notes the lady had received, gently declining the invitation and forcing her to draw a line through the names so hopefully penned. Amelia noted that Earl Rossleigh and Lord Delham had not replied, but she had little hope that either of these gentlemen would put in an appearance. Even the earl's attentions towards Camilla and his outrageous flirting with the young lady did not convince her that his interest was strong enough to bring him to Blenheim Terrace that evening.

With a heavy heart Miss Langridge took her time over her preparations for the party. She had seen Camilla's new gown of yellow silk trimmed with quantities of gold lace and discarded the thought of wearing her apple-green silk again. Instead she instructed her maid to lay out her plum-coloured satin with the white petticoat embroidered with deep red flowers. A narrow flounce of lace ran round the low neckline and Amelia waved away the white fichu that the maid held out for her: it was already warm and she guessed that as the night progressed the house would become even hotter. She put on her fine pearl ear-rings but was disappointed to find that the matching necklace her mother had given her was broken. None of her other trinkets would do and in the end she settled for a narrow band of ribbon that matched her gown, fastened with a neat pearl pin. She stood before the mirror, observing her reflection with a critical eye. The simple lines of her gown flattered her figure, and the ribbon at her neck accentuated the slender column of her throat.

'Very nice, Miss, if I may say so,' offered her maid.

Amelia pulled a face.

'A little plain, perhaps, but it will have to do.'

The family dinner took place in an atmosphere of suppressed excitement. Camilla's only topic of conversation was which gentlemen she should dance with.

'It is too bad that I cannot dance with them all,' she sighed, 'but I do hope that Sir Martyn arrives in time to dance with me. He has promised to try.'

'Sir Martyn Pudsey?' exclaimed Miss Langridge. 'I didn't see his name on the guest list.'

'No,' admitted Mrs Strickland, 'but when we saw him the other night he was so attentive to dear Camilla that she begged me to invite him, which I did, there and then, for as I told him, we stand upon no ceremony here. And he did promise to look in.'

Amelia uttered up a silent prayer of thanks that Lady Isabelle had left Town. Mr Strickland lifted his wine glass.

'Perhaps Miss Langridge has a personal interest in Sir Martyn.'

Amelia's lip curled. Since the duel Mr Strickland's behaviour towards her had been decidedly cool, a fact that she attributed to her own lack of concern for his safety.

'On the contrary,' she told him, 'I cannot like the man, and I would urge Camilla to be very careful where Sir Martyn is concerned.'

Camilla tossed her head.

'You mean to warn me that he is married. Well I know it, and I also know that his wife has left Town. Besides, being married does not prevent him from being a most agreeable dancing partner, and he pays me the most handsome compliments.'

Miss Langridge looked at Mrs Strickland, but she was merely smiling at her daughter, only too pleased that Camilla had added such a rich and powerful gentleman to her list of admirers. With a tiny shake of her head Amelia turned her attention back to her dinner. The evening had never held a great deal of attraction for her, but if Sir Martyn was going to be present, she found herself looking forward to it even less.

The first of the country dances had ended when Miss Langridge noticed a gentleman in a green striped silk coat making his way towards her.

'Lord Delham, I am glad that you could come.' She held out her hand to him, adding quietly, 'When did you get back?'

'Two days since. I looked for you in the park, but was not fortunate enough to see you there.'

'No, my lord. I have been very busy with the preparations for the party and shopping with Miss Strickland.' Shrieks from some of the young ladies on the dance floor made her grimace and she turned away. 'So how did you leave Lady Isabelle?'

'Well, thank you, Miss Langridge. Miss Templecombe is indeed exceedingly kind to her and when I left, my sister was already looking much better for her care, even after such a short time.'

'I am glad. And while she recovers her strength there you may consider a more permanent solution.'

'The best would be to put a bullet through Pudsey's black heart.' he muttered savagely. 'Rossleigh could do it, an he would. He is a crack shot.'

'Yes, I have heard he is an expert at duelling.'

'What's that, ma'am?' Lord Delham's brows rose at the bitterness in her voice. 'Oh of course,' he continued, his brow clearing. 'You're thinking of that little affair between Strickland and Mr Crannock.'

'I was there when the challenge was issued.' Her fingers tightened around the slender sticks of her fan. 'I know it is irregular – you will most likely consider it very wrong of me – but I asked Lord Rossleigh to intervene, to prevent the duel. He would not.'

'My dear ma'am, how could he? From what I have heard the two of them were determined to fight, neither could back down with honour.'

'Honour! What honour is there in killing a man? I find society's ideas of honour very difficult to accept, sir.' She saw he was looking troubled and bit her lip. After a moment she put out her hand, saying with her ready smile, 'I am sorry, my lord, it is none of your concern, and everything ended well, after all.' She gave her head a little shake, as if to cast off her sombre thoughts. 'I must warn you, sir, that Sir Martyn attends this evening.'

'I know. I have already seen him, dancing with Miss Strickland.' He smiled ruefully. 'It means we must not be seen talking for too long, Miss Langridge. I suppose it would be best if we did not dance, either. Forgive me.'

She smiled. 'I will endeavour to bear the disappointment, my lord.'

'And I am sure Ross will remedy my omission, ma'am.'

'Oh, is Lord Rossleigh here?'

'Aye, we came in together, but he was waylaid by old Morrisey, wanting to sell him another horse.'

'Oh, oh I did not expect him to come tonight. . . .'

'Well neither did I, to be honest, Miss Langridge, but he insisted we put in an appearance. Probably pursuing his flirtation with the beautiful Camilla.'

Miss Langridge's smile was a trifle strained.

'Yes, most likely.'

'Good lord, here is Mrs Strickland bearing down upon us, and looking mighty pleased, too.'

'And so she should, with the number of guests crowded into her house.' Her eyes twinkled mischievously. 'Doubtless she will wish to make sure you are well entertained.'

She ignored Lord Delham's whispered protest and excused herself, leaving Mrs Strickland to carry off the young lord and introduce him to some young lady without a partner for the next dance.

Miss Langridge's spirits were oppressed. Although a part of her wanted very much to see Lord Rossleigh, the feeling that he had failed her would not go away. She sighed and admitted to herself how much she liked the earl, and while she told herself that he had acted in accordance with the accepted code of honour governing duels, she knew her depression lay in the fact that she had turned to him for help and he had refused her. When she glimpsed his dark head on the edge of the crowd, she moved in the opposite direction to avoid him.

'Miss Langridge!'

Looking up, she found Simon Lyddon at her side.

'Are you quite well, ma'am? Your countenance is too solemn for a party!'

She forced a smile.

'It is nothing, sir – a slight headache. I-I find the crowded rooms oppressive.'

The gentleman looked concerned and offered to fetch her a glass of wine, but she did not hear him: she had seen Lord Rossleigh bearing down upon her. Desperation made her bold, and she laid her hand on Mr Lyddon's sleeve.

'Listen! They are striking up for the cotillion, will you dance with me?'

'Of course, ma'am, if you wish.'

Even before he had finished speaking she grabbed his hand and almost dragged him into the middle of the dancers.

'But what of your headache, Miss Langridge?'

'Oh, I am sure a little exertion will relieve it.'

Out of the corner of her eye she saw the earl watching her

and she chattered on, smiling in such a determined manner that her cheeks began to ache. Her partner responded gallantly, but there was a speculative light in his eye as he waited for a chance to speak.

'Forgive me, Miss Langridge, but this is not your usual style. Would your sudden desire to dance have something to do with my lord Rossleigh?'

'With the earl! Wh-why should you think that?'

'I think you hurried me out here to avoid him.' Amelia was thankful that the movement of the dance prevented an immediate answer, but Mr Lyddon was not to be distracted. As the music ended he pulled her hand on to his arm. 'Well, Miss Langridge?'

She sighed. 'You are right, Mr Lyddon. I *am* avoiding him.' She looked up, frowning slightly, as if deciding how much to trust him. 'You were your cousin's second at the recent duel, were you not?'

'I was, ma'am. I was sorry that you had to witness the argument.'

'So too am I. To call a man out over such a trifle, it is – it is barbaric. Oh I know that is not how you gentlemen see it, but consider, either one of them might have been killed. I tried to reason with Edmund, but he was in a towering rage and would pay me no heed, so I turned to Lord Rossleigh. You need not tell me my task was fruitless, sir,' she said bitterly. 'I am well aware that once engaged upon a duel, neither party will withdraw, even when their seconds are supposed to be doing everything to avert a meeting.'

He led her to a vacant sofa.

'Miss Langridge, you have to understand – neither man would be moved from his course.'

She nodded. 'I know.'

'And you must allow that it all came to nought.'

'That too I know.'

She looked up, and he was taken aback at the depth of the sorrow in her face.

'It is not the duel, exactly. It is . . . I trusted Lord Rossleigh, I felt sure that he would help me an he could, but when – when I *begged* him to intercede, he would not.'

Mr Lyddon was regarding her steadily. He appeared to be wrestling with himself, for he opened his mouth to speak, then closed it again. Amelia stared down at her hands, wondering if her hostess would allow her to leave the party early. Sitting beside her, Mr Lyddon sighed.

'Miss Langridge, there is something you should know, but not here, it is too public.' He rose and bowed over her hand. 'I will leave you now, ma'am, but if you could slip away and meet me in the morning-room in, say, half an hour, I think I can allay at least some of your anxieties.'

He met her wondering glance with a reassuring smile and walked off. Amelia watched him go, her mind racing as she tried to make sense of all he had said. She jumped when she heard Lord Rossleigh's voice behind her.

'Well, well,' he drawled. 'First Crannock and Strickland, and now you appear to have poor Lyddon dancing attendance upon you. You are to be congratulated, ma'am.'

Startled, she looked round, aware that her cheeks were flushed. She swallowed and tried to speak coolly.

'You are absurd, sir.'

His smile was as wide as ever, but she noticed that his eyes were glittering angrily as he looked down at her.

'Are you avoiding me this evening, Miss Langridge?' He came to sit beside her, resting one arm lightly along the back of the sofa.

She was immediately aware of his hand lying so close to her bare neck; she could even fancy that she felt the air move as his fingers drummed idly on the soft velvet.

'A-avoiding you, my lord? Why should that be?'

'Perhaps you could tell me.'

She closed her eyes: she would gamble everything.

'You did not stop the duel.'

The fingers were stilled.

'Ah, the duel. It was a very tame affair, no one was hurt.'

'No thanks to you.' she retorted, hurt increasing her anger.

'I told you to trust me, madam.'

'Trust you! Oh, I have heard it so many times now, that the bullet seldom hits its target, that they could fire into the air and still honour would be satisfied – but you could not know that.'

He regarded her silently, his smile quite gone.

'I did know it, however.'

'How could you do so?'

'That I cannot tell you.'

She fought down her disappointment.

'Then there is nothing more to say.' She spoke softly, blinking back her tears.

Miss Strickland's playful tones interrupted them.

'My Lord, I have been looking all over for you.' Camilla came up, ignoring Amelia as she turned her expressive dark eyes upon the earl. 'You promised me this dance, my lord, and I am not minded to excuse you.'

Immediately the earl's ready smile returned. He rose, saying lightly, 'And why should you, Miss Strickland? I am at your service.' He took her hand and went off with only the slightest of bows towards Amelia.

It was a simple task for Miss Langridge to slip away from the party and make her way to the morning-room. Apart from the wooden-faced footmen standing silently in the hall, the lower floor was deserted and Amelia was glad to leave the noise and heat of the overcrowded upper rooms for a while. She found Mr Lyddon waiting for her. The gleam from the candles in the wall sconces and the branched candlestick upon the table seemed dull compared to the brilliance of the drawing-room, but it was sufficient for Amelia to see that the gentleman was looking unusually solemn. She spoke without preamble.

'Well, sir, what is it you wish to say to me?'

'I have to break a confidence,' he said, after a slight pause. 'Unfortunate, but I think it is necessary.'

'It is?'

'Yes, for Rossleigh would never tell you himself.'

She moved towards him, frowning a little.

'Tell me what, sir?'

He stood looking at her in silence for a long moment and when at last he spoke it was with some difficulty.

'It is possible that the recent change to my own feelings has allowed me to be more sensitive to others, but I think you are not . . . indifferent to the earl.' He held up his hand as she was about to protest. 'I know that you held him in high esteem until the duel. You believe he refused to help you. Is that not so?'

Silently she nodded.

'Then . . . you must know, Miss Langridge, that he did not ignore your pleas. In fact he risked his own honour for your sake.'

Amelia clasped her hands before her, keeping her eyes on his face.

'Mr Lyddon – I do not understand. . . .'

Mr Lyddon turned away and walked to the fireplace, gazing down into the empty hearth. 'On the morning of the duel Rossleigh and I accompanied Crannock and my cousin to the heath, as is customary. Rossleigh had offered them the use of his duelling pistols, a very fine pair, only ever used in practice and, I should think, deadly accurate.' Miss Langridge put her hands to her cheeks as he continued. 'It is customary for the seconds to confer on such occasions, and to oversee the loading of the weapons, to see fair play. Lord Rossleigh drew me to one side and invited me to join him in loading the pistols. They were beautifully made, Miss Langridge, perfectly balanced. We took the necessary pieces from the case and proceeded to load the pistols – the ramrod, wadding and powder – but no ball.'

The gentleman turned to face Amelia, who was looking puzzled. He went on, 'Rossleigh told me he intended to palm the ball, that is, to put in the powder and the wadding, but without the ball there would be nothing more than the sound coming out when the trigger was squeezed. Completely harmless.'

She stared at him.

'But – but did they not notice?'

Mr Lyddon grinned.

'Lord no, they were both so nervous they could hardly hold the dashed pistols, let alone know there was no shot in them.'

'You – do you mean that he made sure they could not kill each other?'

'Aye, madam, he did, but if this gets out it could ruin him – and me. I must ask for your silence on this matter.'

He watched as she digested this information, noting the heightened colour in her cheek and the sudden glow in her eyes. She went forward to take his hands.

'No, no I promise you I shall not mention this to another soul! Except Lord Rossleigh, of course – I must beg his pardon for—'

Mr Lyddon looked startled.

'On no account must you say a word of this to the earl!' he exclaimed. 'If he knew I had broken my word he would call *me* out for sure. Promise me that you will say nothing to him.'

Reluctantly Amelia agreed. She smiled at him, her eyes shining.

'Thank you, sir. I am forever in your debt.'

He gave her an enigmatic look.

'Perhaps you will be able to help *me*, one day, ma'am.'

'Anything, sir!' she agreed gaily. 'Now, we must get back to the party before Mrs Strickland comes looking for us.'

'Very well. You had best go first, Miss Langridge, and I will follow in a few moments.'

With a final, grateful smile at the gentleman Amelia left the room and made her way quickly back up the stairs, feeling as if a heavy cloud had lifted from her spirits. Conscious of her last unhappy meeting with the earl, she searched through the upper rooms in vain for him. She spotted Camilla dancing with Lord Delham and decided to wait until the dance was ended to ask the young lord where his friend might be. Impatiently she moved about the room, coming at last back to the landing where the sound of a familiar voice in the hallway below caused her to move to the balustrade and peer over. The earl was in the hall, collecting his hat and cape from a footman.

'Lord Rossleigh!' she flew down the stairs, regardless of decorum. 'My lord, you are not going.'

He looked at her, no hint of a smile in his eyes.

'As you see, madam.'

'But – it is early yet. You cannot go.'

'I can, and I will.'

Hurriedly she stepped in front of him, barring his way.

'No, please – please my lord. Do not go like this.'

Her heart sank at his hard look, but she gathered her courage for one final bid.

'Lord Rossleigh, at least talk to me. Will you not step into the morning-room?' She held her breath, afraid he would refuse, but after a long moment he gave a slight nod and stepped aside, that she might precede him. Amelia led the way across the hall, fully aware of the speculation that would be going on behind the basilisk stares of the footmen: to be going into the room alone with a gentleman for a second time would surely give rise to gossip in the servants' hall later that night, when they finished off the bottles of wine and picked over the remains of the supper.

Once the door was firmly shut upon prying eyes and ears, Miss Langridge faced the earl, staring up into his unyielding countenance. Heavens, how was she to placate him without disclosing what Mr Lyddon had told her.

'Well madam, what is it that you wish to say to me?' She winced at his impatient tone. 'You have already made it abundantly clear that you think I have failed you. Pray let us not prolong the charade.'

'That is just it, my lord. I want to – to apologize for doubting you, sir. For not trusting you.' She forced herself to look at him, meeting his stern gaze steadily. 'I would not have you leave without knowing how – how much I . . . value your friendship.'

His eyes narrowed.

'Now what the devil has brought on this change of heart?'

She looked away, aware of the hot colour flooding her cheeks and frightened that he might read her thoughts.

'I could not bear to lose your friendship, my lord. At least tell me you forgive me for doubting you.'

His face softened. 'There is nothing to forgive, Miss Langridge.' The caress in his voice was unmistakable. Amelia looked up quickly and saw him smiling down at her with such tenderness that her heart leapt, hammering painfully against her ribs.

'Does – does that mean we are still friends?' she asked, a little breathlessly.

He took her hands.

'I hope we can be more than that. Amelia—'

A wild elation flooded through her as she anticipated his next words. She was hardly aware of the sound of voices and a hasty step in the hall, but when the door opened the earl released her, stepping away as a testy voice was heard in the doorway.

'Yes, yes, now out of my way!'

Mr Crannock strode in.

'Edmund!' She turned towards him, grateful that the few lighted candles were behind her, and therefore her flushed cheeks would be in shadow.

'Miss Langridge – Amelia, my dear! I came as soon as I could.' He frowned at the earl, aware for the first time of his presence in the room. 'My lord, may I ask why you are here, alone, with Miss Langridge?'

'I was feeling a little faint, Edmund,' Amelia put in quickly. 'Lord Rossleigh was kind enough to escort me here, away from the heat and the crowd.'

Mr Crannock did not look satisfied, but he was obviously labouring under a much greater preoccupation, and he let it pass. Silently the earl withdrew to a corner of the room and watched Mr Crannock turn once again to Amelia.

'My dear, I think you should sit down. I have some bad news for you.'

'Oh? From – from Langridge Court?'

'Yes, my poor child. A servant arrived scarcely a half-hour since. I had just got in from my lecture when he called.'

She raised her hand to interrupt him.

'But, if it is from home, why did he not come to see me?'

Mr Crannock possessed himself of her hands.

'He was on his way here, my dear, but I told him there was no need. I preferred to bring you your mama's note myself. I thought you would want to hear the news from someone close to you.'

She shook her head at him and said a little impatiently, 'Edmund what is it – Grandpapa?'

'Alas, yes.' He bowed his head. 'Lord Langridge contracted

a chill a few days ago. He died last night. I am sorry.'

'Oh.'

He guided her to a chair, and hovered over her.

'You are grieved, my dear, but not, I hope, prostrate. Lord Langridge was an old man and this cannot be unexpected. But now – as your grandfather's heir your place is at home – my lady.'

'My lady!' Lord Rossleigh exclaimed.

Mr Crannock looked around.

'Oh, are you still here? Yes, she is now Baroness Langridge of Langridge Court.'

'The devil she is.' The earl looked at her, his crooked smile appearing briefly. 'Amelia, you wretch, why did you try to gammon me that you were not of my world?'

Mr Crannock straightened and glared disapprovingly at the earl.

'My lord, she became a lady at midnight.'

'She has always been a lady,' muttered Lord Rossleigh.

The lady rose, squaring her shoulders.

'I must go to my family. Edmund, pray find Mrs Strickland, explain to her what has happened.' She saw him hesitate and gave him a little push. 'Go, Edmund. I will join you presently.' She ushered him out of the room and closed the door behind him, then she turned to look at the earl. 'Mama will need me at Langridge Court.'

'Of course. You will leave at dawn?'

'Yes. I must go now and pack. Please tell Lord Delham and your sister. I would not have them think me so discourteous as to leave Town without a word.'

He came towards the door.

'They will understand.' He took her hand, lifting it to his lips. 'God speed, my lady.'

Her fingers tightened around his, and for one wild moment she wanted to beg him to come with her, but it could not be.

She had no right to ask that of him, and there was no need, after all: Edmund would provide sufficient escort. She raised her chin, summoning all her strength to give him one last smile.

'Thank you. Goodbye, my lord.' With one last swift, dipping curtsy she turned and swept from the room.

Chapter Fifteen

*A*melia would have been gratified to know how many people remarked her absence during the weeks that followed her departure. She had never courted popularity, and had been content to go about in the shadow of Camilla's dazzling presence, but her kindly nature and calm good sense had had its effect and many of Camilla's young admirers missed having her sympathetic ear to listen to their woes, and their mamas were chagrined to learn that the demure Miss Langridge that they had dismissed as merely a companion to Miss Strickland was now Baroness Langridge – if they had known, they would most certainly have directed their foolish sons to pay more attention to one whom they had always thought to be a very pretty-behaved young woman. To those who enquired after Miss Langridge, Mrs Strickland made the proper answers but she was too concerned with her daughter's success to spare more than a passing thought for anyone else. Miss Strickland still had numerous admirers, but very few of them could be considered a brilliant catch. Passing them all under review, Mrs Strickland knew a momentary disappointment at the lack of noblemen amongst their ranks. Lord Delham's early infatuation had soon worn off, and although Lord Rossleigh could be relied upon to claim Camilla's hand at every ball and to pay her handsome compliments, Mrs Strickland was shrewd enough to realize that the earl had no intention of entering into anything more serious than a flirtation. Her eyes narrowed as she considered if it would be possible to force the earl into marriage, but soon gave up the idea. Lord Rossleigh had been on the Town for several years and numerous caps had been thrown at him, all to no avail. He was alive to every suit and although he was unfailingly courteous and good-humoured, Mrs Strickland had occasionally glimpsed the steel in his eyes that warned her he would not be caught in her wiles, and she was canny enough not to risk her daughter's humiliation by attempting to set a trap for him.

That left only Sir Martyn Pudsey. He was rich, powerful and clearly hot for Camilla, but he was a married man. Mrs Strickland had heard rumours that Lady Pudsey had disappeared and her observations of Sir Martyn's behaviour had not led her to believe he was too concerned in finding his wife. Watching his attentions to her daughter, Mrs Strickland began to grow more hopeful. Camilla was a clever little puss who knew how to please a man such as Sir Martyn: if she kept her head and followed her mama's advice Sir Martyn could be persuaded to put aside his errant wife in favour of a much more agreeable bride.

Chapter Sixteen

$\mathcal{L}$ord Rossleigh groaned quietly as his valet threw back the hangings about his bed.

'A very good morning to you, my lord, and might I say what a fine morning it is, an' all!'

'Damn you, O'Brien. What time is it?'

'Ten o'clock, my lord. You are engaged to take Lady Charlotte driving at noon.'

Lord Rossleigh grunted and while the valet busied himself pulling various items of clothing from a large press he slipped out of bed and plunged his head into the bowl of water on the stand. O'Brien waited patiently until the earl had dried his face then handed him a fine lawn shirt. 'Did I tell you, sir, that I had word from my nephew yesterday?'

'Which one would that be? You have such a large family I find it difficult to remember them all.'

O'Brien grinned. 'Aye, sir, that I have. Your lordship might recall I told you some time ago about Patrick, my eldest sister's boy.'

'Would that be the bank clerk, O'Brien?' said the earl, standing before the mirror.

'The very same, my lord. Patrick's a fine boy, so he is, and very quick. His masters at the bank seem very pleased with him, and he works very hard, adding up the accounts, counting out the shillings and generally tidying up for his betters.'

He helped the earl into his waistcoast. 'Aye, sir, A very obser-vant lad is Patrick, and he just happened to be tidying one of the desks when he sees a ledger bearing the name of Sir Martyn Pudsey.'

Lord Rossleigh paused as he straightened his shirt.

'Interesting that your – er – Patrick should find himself a place with Pudsey's bankers.' In the mirror his eyes met the innocent glance of his valet.

'Aye, my lord, quite a coincidence, I'm thinking.'

'Go on. Was the ledger open, perhaps?'

'As to that sir, young Patrick didn't say, but one would assume so, for it would not do for him to be snooping around in the office, now would it?'

'Definitely not,' murmured the earl, putting out his hand. The valet handed him a neckcloth. 'Well?'

'Well, my lord, young Patrick noticed that amongst all the general entries there is a regular payment from the bank.' He paused as the earl concentrated on knotting his neck-cloth, then he helped him into a frockcoat of plum-coloured velvet embroidered richly with gold.

'Go on, man!'

O'Brien picked up the earl's jewel box.

'May I suggest the ruby pin, sir, with that coat?'

The earl ignored him.

'A regular payment? Was there a name?'

'Aye, sir. It is to a Mr Jameson, in Keynsham.'

The earl's eyes gleamed.

'Keynsham? O'Brien, you interest me. I have been thinking for some time that we should go out of Town for a while; it is devilish thin of company at this time o' year. What do you say to Bath?'

'Bath, sir? Whist now, it's not as fashionable as it was, but I believe it is still considered an entertainin' place.'

The earl nodded, a slight smile curving his lips.

'Indeed, and it is very close to Keynsham, I understand.'

'Is it now? Well, I don't know too much about that, but if your lordship says so I'm sure it is so.'

Lord Rossleigh studied his reflection in the mirror.

'It is also close to Langridge Court,' he murmured.

A smile lurked in the valet's shrewd eyes.

'Aye, I believe it is that. Now, my lord – the ruby?'

The stable yard at Langridge Court was a perfect square, built of the same honey-coloured stone as the house, with arched openings on two sides, one leading out into the landscaped park, the other curving towards the main drive. Amelia entered from the park on her long-tailed bay and trotted across to the large double doors where her grim-faced groom was waiting for her, his eyes narrowed against the glare of the midday sun. She smiled down at him.

'Oh dear, am I late, Yatton?'

The groom put his hand up to catch the bay's bridle while the lady slid nimbly to the ground.

'You said you'd be no more'n an hour, my lady,' he growled. 'Mr Crannock rode over and waited for you, but he's gone now.'

'I know, I saw him ride in – that's why I decided to take another turn in the park. Pray don't scold me, Yatton,' she implored him, 'I know it was wrong of me, but I did not want to listen to him commiserating with me again – he has said it all before – several times now. I know he means well, but his sermonizing makes me want to fly off and do something quite outrageous!'

The groom's weather-beaten face softened.

'Aye, you never could bear sympathy, could you, Miss Amelia? You leave the mare with me and seek out your poor mama. She's had the entertaining of the gentleman for the past half-hour.'

Not waiting to change out of her riding habit, Amelia hurried to the yellow saloon where she found Mrs Langridge engaged at her needlework. She was wearing deep mourning, and the embroidery was a welcome splash of colour against the severe black gown. Mrs Langridge looked up as her daughter entered.

'So there you are: I was about to send Yatton to search for you.'

'Mama, you know you never worry about me when I ride in the park,' said Amelia, coming up to plant a kiss on her brow. 'It was such a fine day that I did not wish to come back indoors. Forgive me!'

Mrs Langridge was not proof against her coaxing tone but she tried her best to look severe.

'You know I do not like you to be out in the heat of the day. Edmund was here. He waited for you for nearly an hour.'

'Then I am sorry, Mama, if you had to bear with his dull prosing.'

'Amelia, how can you be so unkind, when you know he has been such a support to us during this sad time?'

'A support!' Amelia drew a breath, fighting down her retort. 'I am sorry, Mama, and I *am* grateful, but he presumes too much. He has become most possessive since Grandpapa died, and no matter how much I try to tell him, he will not believe I have no intention of marrying him.'

'Well. . . .'

Something in her mother's tone made Amelia look at her sharply.

'Mama, I hope you have not encouraged him to think I will wed him.'

'But it was your grandfather's wish, my love.'

'But not his command.' Shaking her head, Amelia looked out of the window, where the great park stretched invitingly to the horizon. 'Do you not see, Mama, we would drive each other to distraction within a month.'

'Well, I had hoped that your stay in London would prove more fruitful,' remarked Mrs Langridge, unable to hide a note of disappointment.

For an instant Amelia pictured Lord Rossleigh's smiling face. She shut her eyes: she would not encourage such foolishness, it was after all many weeks since she had left London and she had heard nothing from the earl.

'Alas, no suitor appeared, Mama. But one thing my time in Town has taught me, I *cannot* marry Edmund.'

Mrs Langridge knew well her daughter's stubborn streak and forbore to press her. Instead she tried to divert her by suggesting they drive to Bath the following day.

'It would not do to be frivolous, of course,' she added anxiously, 'but there are several purchases I must make and no one could object if we visited the Pump Rooms.'

Amelia's eyes twinkled.

'Of course, Mama. And it is always possible that you will find acquaintances there and enjoy a little gossip. By all means let us go. It will give me the opportunity to wear my new black crepe. In fact.' She paused, throwing a speculative glance towards Mrs Langridge. 'Mama, would you object if I did not accompany you to the Pump Rooms? If you would allow me to drop you at the White Lion, I would very much like to drive on to Midford and call upon Miss Templecombe. It is such a long time since we met and she wrote such a kind letter to me after Grandpapa's death that I would dearly like to see her.'

Mrs Langridge was too pleased to see the animation in her daughter to object. It was two months since Baron Langridge's death, and the ladies had remained very much at home with only the daily visits of Edmund Crannock to relieve the monotony of their days. They had busied themselves with clearing the late lord's apartments and replying to the many letters of condolence. Adding this to the running of the estate and looking after the house, there was plenty to do, but Mrs Langridge noted with dismay the continuing pallor of Amelia's cheek and the almost dreamlike way she went about her tasks.

Thus is was that the Langridge carriage was ordered the following morning and carried the two ladies, suitably veiled, through the leafy lanes to Bath, where Amelia parted from her mother. Amelia was aware that her visit to Midford could not be a long one, but since she had suggested sending Lady Isabelle to stay with her old governess, she was anxious to assure herself that everything was well. Miss Templecombe's letter of condolence had made vague references to her young visitor and Amelia had been wondering how she could visit Midford alone: she had been very much afraid that if she proposed riding over to see Miss Templecombe her mama would insist that Mr Crannock should accompany her, and she knew he would ask questions. Now, as the carriage rumbled into the little village, she waited eagerly for her first glimpse of Miss Templecombe's modest cottage. Her fears that by arriving unannounced she might find her old governess from home were soon proved groundless. She was admitted to the tiny sitting-room where Miss Templecombe was waiting to greet her. The lady was tall and spare, but her kindly face and twinkling grey eyes had won the heart of many a shy pupil and now she held out her arms to Amelia.

'My poor child.'

With a sound halfway between a sob and a laugh Amelia threw herself into those arms.

'Oh my dear Miss T. how I have missed you! Such a deal of sadness we have had, and without your ready wit to enliven the evenings we have been so dreadfully dull.'

Miss Templecome held Amelia away from her and studied

her face through narrowed eyes.

'You are a trifle more pale than I would like, my love. But that is only natural, after all, when you have suffered such a sad loss. How is your dear mama? Come and sit with me: you must tell me everything and I shall ring for Betty to bring in the tea tray.'

The two ladies immediately fell into comfortable conversation and it was some time before Amelia recalled the purpose of her visit.

'You wrote in your letter how much you were enjoying your young friend's visit – you mean Lady Isabelle, of course – and is that really so? Has her brother not made other plans for her?'

'No, not as yet, but I cannot think it a bad thing. While she is with me Lady Isabelle grows stronger daily and she is quite safe, you know. We live very retired here and my neighbours think she is one of my old pupils, come to visit.' Miss Templecombe's ready smile appeared. 'I have been at pains to allow them to think that'

'Miss T. you are too good! But where is your guest? I had thought to find her with you when I arrived.'

For the first time Miss Templecombe looked faintly uncomfortable.

'She is out walking. It was such a fine day, I saw no objection. . . .'

'Alone? Is that wise, even here?'

'No, no she is not alone. That is. . . .'

They heard Lady Isabelle's merry laugh and a moment later the lady entered the room. Amelia found it difficult to believe that this fresh-faced laughing young beauty could be the same Lady Isabelle she had seen last in Town. The bruises were gone, the haunted look had left her eyes, and the country air had added a peach-like bloom to her cheeks. Her eyes were sparkling as she stepped into the room and speech bubbled forth from her lips.

'Miss T. you will never guess – oh, Miss Langridge!'

But Amelia was not listening to her. The smile of greeting was frozen on her face when she recognized Lady Isabelle's escort.

'Mr Lyddon!'

For a few moments no one spoke. Lady Isabelle's laughter died away and she shrank towards Simon Lyddon, her eyes anxiously watching Miss Langridge.

'I had no idea,' murmured Amelia.

Mr Lyddon gently propelled Lady Isabelle to a chair.

'No, ma'am,' he said, 'I am sure you did not.'

'Mr Lyddon has been a regular visitor,' remarked Miss Templecombe. 'His visits have been very beneficial in raising my lady's spirits.'

Amelia could only stare.

'It is all my fault.' exclaimed Lady Isabelle. 'I-I gave Mr Lyddon my direction before leaving Town. I know it was very wrong of me, Miss Langridge. Henry and Ross both said I should tell no one, but . . .' She dabbed at her eyes with a wisp of lace.

Mr Lyddon fell on his knees before her and proffered his own linen handkerchief.

'Hush, madam, do not upset yourself. Miss Langridge does not blame you.' His eyes took in the black crepe. 'Your pardon – Lady Langridge, I should say.'

Amelia brushed this aside.

'But, but what does this mean? I don't understand. . . .'

'W-we became friends in Town,' whispered Lady Isabelle. 'While I was staying with you – Mrs Strickland is Simon – Mr Lyddon's – aunt, you see. And, and we—'

'We fell in love!' declared Mr Lyddon.

'Oh heavens.'

Miss Templecombe smiled slightly at Amelia's horrified face.

'I admit I did not like the idea when Isabelle first told me, but the damage was done before ever she came to Midford, and it seems cruel to keep them apart.'

Amelia rubbed her temples, trying to think clearly.

'I take it your brother knows nothing of this – and Lord Rossleigh?'

Lady Isabelle shook her head, setting her golden curls dancing.

'Oh no, no one is aware of it, save Miss Templecombe, and now you, of course. Did you see Henry before you left Town, ma'am? How is he, and Lord Rossleigh?'

Amelia could hardly understand the lady's questions for her mind was whirling, but she did her best to answer, and to join in the conversation until a glance at the clock told her it was time to be leaving.

'I, too, must be returning to Bath,' announced Mr Lyddon. 'Pray allow me to escort you, my lady. My horse is in a nearby barn and can be ready in a few minutes.'

'Th-thank you, Mr Lyddon,' Amelia answered mechanically, and during the journey back to Bath she found herself unable to stop her thoughts from racing ahead, envisaging the dangerous consequences of Mr Lyddon's attraction to Lady Isabelle. To hide Sir Martyn's wife from him was bad enough, but to encourage her to take a lover! She blushed at the thought and began to wish that she had not become embroiled in this dangerous game. Then she remembered the night Lord Delham had brought his sister to her: the gaunt face, the frightened expression in her eyes and the livid bruises on her body. She could not regret helping her, and whatever the cost she must see it through. She glanced out of the window at Mr Lyddon's upright figure riding beside the carriage. She knew him for a penniless gambler, but he had a kind heart, and if he truly loved Isabelle then she hoped they would find happiness.

The Langridge coach swept into the yard of the White Hart, slowing to avoid the crush of carts, carriages, horses and stable-hands that jostled for space. Mr Lyddon quickly dismounted and threw the reins to an ostler before striding across to hand Amelia down from the carriage.

'Is this where you are to meet your mama?'

'Yes.' She smiled up at him. 'Thank goodness we ordered a private parlour: there seems to be even more people arriving. Let us go inside: I am sure we will find Mama there.' She tucked her hand in his arm and allowed him to force a passage through the crush of porters and stable-hands until they reached the door to the inn, but as Mr Lyddon stood back to allow her to precede him she found the way blocked by a large gentleman in a many-caped driving coat. He had his back to her and his broad shoulders filled the narrow corridor.

'Make way for the lady, sir.'

Amelia paused as Mr Lyddon's impatient words reverberated from the narrow walls. The gentlemen turned and for the second time that day she found herself bereft of speech as she found herself facing Earl Rossleigh.

Chapter Seventeen

$\mathcal{A}$melia saw the momentary gleam of surprise and pleasure in the earl's hard eyes, but it was replaced almost immediately with a more measured look: Mr Lyddon had stepped into the passage behind her to avoid the crowds outside, and she knew he was standing much closer to her than was seemly, but there was nothing she could do. The earl raised his hat.

'Miss L— your pardon. *Lady* Langridge, your servant, ma'am. And Mr Lyddon, an – ah – unexpected pleasure.' The sarcasm was thinly veiled, but it occurred to Amelia that his displeasure might be caused by jealousy. The thought gave her courage.

'Lord Rossleigh.' She made herself meet his frowning eyes. 'Are you just arrived in Bath?'

The landlord's cough made her look beyond the earl.

'Your private parlour is ready for you, my lady, if you would step this way. . . . ?'

She nodded and smiled at Lord Rossleigh.

'Will you not join us, sir, just for a moment, I fear we are blocking the passageway.'

With a brief nod he turned and they all followed the landlord to a small parlour opposite the taproom. Mr Lyddon hung back, reluctant to join them but the lady gave him a warning glance and obliged him to accompany her.

155

'Well, that is much better,' she remarked, as the landlord closed the door upon them, shutting out the worst of the noise. 'I have arranged to meet my mother here, Lord Rossleigh and – and I would be honoured if you would allow me to make you known to her.'

'The honour would be mine, my lady.'

She gave him a bright smile.

'I have been to Midford this morning, and Mr Lyddon kindly agreed to escort me back to Bath – I understand Mr Lyddon has been in the habit of visiting Lady Isabelle.'

'The devil he has!'

'I think it is one of the reasons she has been so content to remain with Miss Templecombe,' she continued quickly, adding with a smile at Mr Lyddon, 'I think it best to be honest with Lord Rossleigh, sir. I hope you do not object.'

The earl gave a short laugh.

'It would make little difference if you did object, Lyddon.'

Simon Lyddon had moved across to the window, frowning heavily.

'Lady Isabelle told me of your kindness to her, Rossleigh, but I see no reason to account to you for my actions.'

'None at all,' agreed the earl. 'My only object is to keep the lady and her brother safe from Pudsey's wrath, and any thoughts he may have of revenge.'

'If I could I would take her out of the country. It would be easy to lose ourselves in France, or Italy.'

'I doubt her brother would agree to the scheme.'

'I am sure Mr Lyddon would not wish to endanger the lady,' put in Amelia, untying the strings of her bonnet.

'Of course not.'

'Then it would be better if he were not in Bath.'

Mr Lyddon threw a challenging look towards the earl.

'As far as my friends and family are concerned, I am here to visit an aged relative.'

'Oh, would that be Camilla's grandmother? Miss Strickland was staying with her in March, I believe, before we travelled to London together.'

Mr Lyddon allowed himself a slight smile.

'Aye, she is my grandmother too. My Aunt Strickland insists upon a show of family loyalty, in the hope that the old lady can be persuaded to leave her money to Camilla and her brother. Unfortunately, all she does is come to blows with her: Grandmama never approved of my uncle Strickland's choice of wife and they always get to cap-pulling if they are together for any length of time.'

'If I can bring you back to more pressing matters,' the earl's voice cut in, impatience lending an edge to his tone. 'Lyddon, how long do you intend to stay in Bath?'

'What is that to you?'

'Everything, since I am attempting to extricate Lady Isabelle from this damned coil.'

'Then I want to help you.'

Lady Langridge gave him an admiring look.

'That is exceedingly noble of you, Mr Lyddon.'

'Exceedingly inconvenient!' snapped the earl. 'Lord Delham and I are best left to deal with this matter alone.'

'Isabelle has told me everything.' declared Mr Lyddon, bristling.

'More fool her.'

The baroness stepped forward.

'That is enough!' she said in her sternest tone. 'Since everyone's desire is to protect Lady Isabelle, arguing over the matter is scarcely helpful. My lord, if Lady Isabelle has taken Mr Lyddon into her confidence then I think you should trust him, too, and allow him to help you.'

'Secrecy is vital to our plans.'

'And Mr Lyddon has done nothing to jeopardize that.' She put out her hand and cast an appealing glance up at the earl.

'He truly loves her, my lord, and he could be a useful ally.' Absently he put his hand over her fingers as they rested on his arm. 'Come,' she coaxed him, 'accept his help, my lord.'

Lord Rossleigh gazed down at her for a long moment and she was relieved to see the frown leaving his eyes. Finally he nodded.

'Very well, it is better that we all work together.' He held out his hand to Mr Lyddon. 'Let me know your direction, sir. Lord Delham arrives in Bath tomorrow and we will meet then to discuss what is to be done.'

Lady Langridge stifled a sigh: there was never any question that she should join their discussions, and she acknowledged to herself how desperately she wanted to be involved.

'And here is Mama coming in now.' she exclaimed, looking out of the window. 'That is very timely, for a moment earlier and we would have had to curtail this conversation.' She moved forward to open the door for Mrs Langridge and at the same time called for coffee to be brought in. Mrs Langridge was somewhat surprised to find her daughter closeted with two gentlemen, both of them unknown to her, and when they were introduced she immediately became prey to the wildest conjecture that Amelia, who had returned from London declaring that she had attracted no suitors, should be on such friendly terms with two such fashionable gentlemen. It was not to be expected that Mrs Langridge would keep her suspicions to herself and Amelia had a very trying half-hour during the drive back to Langridge Court explaining the presence of two such gentlemen in Bath without disclosing Lady Isabelle's story.

'Well,' exclaimed her mama, 'I cannot condone your behaviour in inviting the gentlemen to join you at the White Hart without even a maid present, but they are both very pleasant gentlemen and I shall be very happy to welcome them to Langridge Court.'

'Mama, I wish you had not invited them.'

'And pray why not? Just because we are in mourning does not mean we must live like hermits. They understand very well that we do not entertain, but Lord Rossleigh seemed particularly eager to call, and if he is happy to visit and to ride about the park with you it will be a very pleasant diversion for you.'

The young baroness compressed her lips.

'I will not see him!'

Mrs Langridge's expressive eyes, twinkled at this petulant statement.

'As you wish, my love.'

Two days later a note arrived at Langridge Court announcing that the earl intended to call upon them the following day. Mr Crannock was with the ladies when the note was delivered and a look of displeasure crossed his features when Mrs Langridge read it aloud.

'It is to be regretted that you have to endure such a visit at this time,' he said heavily. 'One would have thought that your circumstances would have protected you from such importunities, but the likes of Earl Rossleigh have no sense of what is proper. I fear it is a result of Miss Langridge – Lady Langridge, I should say – having gone to Town. . . .'

'You need not be so concerned for us, Edmund,' remarked Mrs Langridge, shaking her head at him. 'Lord Rossleigh seems to be a very pleasant gentleman and I have no doubt his visit will do us no harm.'

'What time does he say he will call, ma'am? I will make sure I am on hand.'

'Why on earth should you do that, Edmund?' exclaimed Amelia. 'You have already told us that you were planning to spend tomorrow with your estate manager. I thought you were to discuss ploughing up your seven-acre field?'

159

'Yes, I had arranged that, but if Lord Rossleigh is coming here—'

'If Lord Rossleigh is coming here it is because I promised to show him over the park,' retorted Amelia, two spots of angry colour blazing on her cheeks. 'And let me tell you, Edmund, that you would be very much in the way.'

Mr Crannock flushed. 'My apologies, madam, if you think I presume too much.'

'Oh no, Edmund,' murmured Mrs Langridge.

'Yes, Edmund!' declared Lady Langridge, looking him in the eye.

Mr Crannock rose.

'Very well, I understand how it is,' he said stiffly. 'My apologies for importuning you. Good day to you, Amelia – Mrs Langridge.'

'Oh dear,' sighed Mrs Langridge when he had left them, closing the door with a snap behind him. 'Poor Edmund, I fear you have wounded him greatly.'

'Nonsense, he will stay away for a day or two and then make his way back, convinced that we cannot go on without him.'

'Amelia!'

'I am sorry, Mama, but he makes me so cross. Lord Rossleigh has proved a better friend than Edmund could ever know.' She flushed and shook her head at her mother's bemused look. 'Pray put that out of your mind, Mama, for I am not at liberty to tell you more, at least not yet, since it concerns the code of honour held so dear by gentlemen. And as for the rest, I promise that I will make it up with Edmund: when I see him again I will ask his advice on pollarding the willows in the south field.'

Despite their harsh words, Lady Langridge half-expected to find Mr Crannock waiting for her in the stable yard the following morning when she walked out from the house with

Lord Rossleigh. There was no sign of him, however and a few minutes later she was trotting out of the yard on her long-tailed bay, admiring the raw-boned hunter that the earl was riding.

'A beautiful creature, my lord. I do not remember seeing him in London?'

'No, I keep Trojan on my estates near Banbury, but I sent word for the groom to bring him to Bath.'

'Once we are clear of the buildings there is a stretch of open ground where we can enjoy a gallop.'

'Will you show me the way, madam?'

'No need,' she threw over her shoulder as she kicked her mare on. 'It's a clear route as far as the home wood on the hill yonder.'

She urged her bay mare forward, but was not surprised when the earl thundered past, turf flying from the hunter's big hooves. The earl drew rein in the shadow of the trees, and waited for the baroness to come up to him.

'Are you too warm, madam, perhaps you would like to rest?'

'No, I am not such a poor creature.' She put up her black veil to display her shining eyes and cheeks becomingly flushed. 'You can have no notion how I have longed to ride like that.'

His lips twitched.

'Not quite the behaviour of a lady in mourning, madam.'

'My grandfather was a great rider in his day, I do not think he would object.' She pointed to a lane leading between the trees. 'Let us take the path through the wood; it leads down to the river, then it will bring us back on the far side of the house.'

The earl nodded and brought Trojan alongside the bay.

'Do you know, my lady, I am a little surprised that you are riding out alone with me today?'

'I need no other escort, my lord, when I have Yatton with me.'

The earl glanced back at the groom riding at a respectful distance behind them.

'I expected the estimable Mr Crannock to be in attendance.'

The words were lightly spoken, but Amelia knew he was watching her. She chose her next words carefully.

'Edmund is a good neighbour, and has been a close family friend for all my life, but he will never be more than that, my lord.' She raised her eyes and found him regarding her with an unusually sober look.

'You relieve my mind, Lady Langridge.'

Amelia became aware of the tension between them and knew a moment of panic. She took refuge in a shaky laugh.

'How strange that sounds! I am not yet grown accustomed to being Lady Langridge. But tell me now – is Lord Delham in Bath, has he seen his sister?'

'Yes, and yes. I have also told him of Lyddon's involvement. He does not like it, of course, but the change it has wrought in his sister, and Miss Templecombe's commendation have done much to reconcile him to the affair, in some part at least. The three of us sat at dinner last night, discussing the matter.'

'And what was decided?'

'Very little. I have information on Pudsey that leads me to Keynsham. If it is as damning as I suspect, then Pudsey is ruined and Isabelle will be free of him.' He put up a hand. 'Please, madam, ask me nothing more yet. I have only conjecture, no proof. You must trust me a little longer.'

'I do, but it irks me that I cannot take more part in this.'

'You have already done more than enough. I would not have Pudsey suspect you are involved; it could put you in danger.'

She waved her hand.

'No more so than you, and I am far less at risk than Lady Isabelle.' She sighed. 'Our mourning restricts my movements, but we will be attending the service at the Abbey on Sunday. Will you be there? We could speak again then.'

Lord Rossleigh jerked on the reins, making the hunter prance across the ground.

'You would have me wait until then to see you again, when I have your mother's consent to take pot luck here whenever I wish?'

Amelia tried to frown and failed.

'You have exerted your charm there to good effect, my lord. I fear my poor mama is quite bewitched.'

'Do you think so?' His crooked grin appeared. 'Then let us return and I shall see if she can be persuaded to invite me to stay for dinner.'

When Amelia awoke on Sunday morning it seemed as though the sun was shining brighter than usual. She hurried downstairs to join her mama at the breakfast-table, humming quietly as she chose her food from the array of silver dishes on the sideboard.

Mrs Langridge looked up from her own meal, smiling.

'You are very cheerful this morning my love.'

'It is a very fine day.'

'It will be white hot in Bath. The streets will be unbearable.'

'But the Abbey is always cool, Mama.'

'Well, be sure to take your fan, child. It would not do to faint off during the sermon.'

Amelia laughed at this, her sunny mood unimpaired. She even managed a smile when Mr Crannock rode up to the door just as they were leaving the house.

'Good morning, Edmund.' Mrs Langridge greeted him. 'We

are on our way to the Abbey.'

'Indeed, then I am in time to accompany you,' he declared, tipping his hat. His glance at Lady Langridge was faintly challenging but Amelia merely smiled at him before climbing into the carriage.

When they reached Bath Mr Crannock gallantly escorted the ladies into the Abbey, where Amelia cast a quick glance around the congregation. Lord Rossleigh's tall figure was not to be seen and she found her good humour waning as she sat patiently through the long service and tedious sermon. At last it was over and they moved outside, where the serious business of social interaction began. Amelia's spirits revived as she saw the earl and Lord Delham approaching. Introductions were made, condolences given and accepted and the gentlemen turned to accompany the ladies back to their carriage. Since Lady Langridge was flanked by the Lords Rossleigh and Delham, it fell to Mr Crannock to offer his arm to Mrs Langridge, who accepted gratefully.

'Tell me, sir,' she said to him, as they followed Amelia and her escorts through the hot streets. 'Is Lord Delham married?'

'No, ma'am.'

'And . . . Lord Rossleigh?'

'He, too, is unmarried.'

The lady's eyes twinkled.

'Dear me,' she murmured, casting a mischievous glance up at the stern face of her escort. 'I did not realize my daughter was on such good terms with so many eligible gentlemen.'

Strolling a little way in front, Amelia asked Lord Delham if he had been to Midford. He nodded.

'I have to say I am delighted with the progress there, except for the presence of a certain gentleman. However, our hostess assures me that Lyddon has been instrumental in my sister's recovery – certainly her spirits are higher than they have been for a very long time.'

'It is a complication,' she agreed, ' but there is nothing to be gained by opposing their friendship at present. I plan to ride that way myself later this week. Perhaps I shall see you then?'

'Perhaps, although Ross and I are careful not to head that way too often.' He stopped as they reached the Langridge carriage and waited for Mrs Langridge and Mr Crannock to come up. As they did so, Lord Rossleigh bent his smile upon the lady.

'I have procured tickets for the concert on Wednesday, madam. It is Handel, quite unexceptional. I hope you and Lady Langridge will be able to join my party?'

Mr Crannock cleared his throat.

'That is kind of you, Rossleigh, but—'

'We would be delighted to accept!' put in Mrs Langridge quickly. 'I am sure there can be no objection to our joining you. Mr Handel's music is always so . . . uplifting.'

Mr Crannock turned away, stopping beside Amelia to say stiffly, 'If I had known that you were ready for jauntering all over Bath—'

'Edmund, it is a *concert*, not a grand ball! Poor Mama has been confined at the Court for long enough. Such a diversion will do much to raise her spirits.' And my own, she added silently.

Mr Crannock scowled, but he said no more, and soon walked off to collect his horse.

Lord Rossleigh was waiting to hand Amelia into the carriage.

'Until Wednesday, ma'am. I have business that will take me out of town until then, so it is unlikely I shall be able to call upon you.'

She smiled to cover her disappointment and allowed her mama to say all that was proper.

'Well, my dear, I think you have not been quite open with me,' said Mrs Langridge when the carriage finally moved off. 'You gave me to understand you had met no eligible gentlemen in Town, yet here you are on the best of terms with three such men in the space of a week, and two of them lords at that!'

'But Mama, they are merely acquaintances. I met them here by the purest chance.'

'It is not mere chance that brought Lord Rossleigh to the Court to go riding with you. Before that I find you drinking coffee with him and Mr Lyddon and today here is Lord Delham greeting you as an old friend. Would you have me believe that they did not come to Bath to see you?'

'Yes I would. Mr Lyddon is here to visit his grandmother.'

'Oh? And the earl, and Lord Delham?'

Since it was impossible to divulge the real reason for their appearance in Bath without revealing Lady Isabelle's story, Amelia merely shrugged and left her mama to indulge in extremely pleasant daydreams involving large settlements and expensive wedding gowns.

Mr Crannock resumed his daily visits, exerting himself so much to please the ladies with newspapers from London and proposals for their entertainment that Amelia found it impossible to rebuff him. She therefore gave up any plans of visiting Lady Isabelle at the beginning of the week and allowed herself to look forward to the concert on Wednesday evening. A rainy day had dispelled the oppressive heat of the city and the concert rooms were pleasantly cool when the ladies arrived to find Lord Rossleigh awaiting them in the vestibule. His frock coat of midnight-blue uncut velvet was embellished with gold frogging, a diamond pin glinted from the snowy ruffles that frothed beneath his chin and another was fastened to the ribbon that held back his unpowdered hair. More ruffles hung over his hands, which were bare of ornament save for a single heavy gold ring. Amelia knew he was not the most lavishly dressed gentleman there, but she thought him by far the most striking and knew a moment of heart-stopping pride when he turned to greet them.

As he approached, she noticed that he was looking unusually solemn. His bow was perfectly correct, but she was both surprised and disappointed when he did not kiss her hand. She was wondering if she had in some way offended when she became aware of a large gentleman in green and scarlet watching them from across the room. Turning her head, she found herself looking into the piercing eyes of Sir Martyn Pudsey.

Chapter Eighteen

She knew Sir Martyn has seen her look of surprise and the slight bow of recognition that he made sent a chill tingling down her spine.

'You have seen Pudsey is here.'

The earl's words were barely audible as he handed Amelia a programme.

'Yes. Lady Isabelle?

'Safe. I believe he is here because of other enquiries I am making.' He took his seat beside Mrs Langridge, leaving Amelia to study the programme, while from the corner of her eye she watched the green and scarlet suit. To her horror she realized that Sir Martyn was approaching. She did not look up, schooling herself to remain calm when he took the vacant seat beside her.

'Ah, Miss Langridge – Baroness,' he corrected himself. 'My condolences, ma'am. I knew your grandfather, years ago, when he was in better health.' The lady inclined her head. 'He died, what – two months ago? A very trying time for you, but no doubt you have the support of your . . . close friends.' His eyes shifted to the earl, who was conversing with Mrs Langridge as if unaware of Sir Martyn's presence. Amelia felt herself blushing and was thankful that the start of the concert made it unnecessary to answer, but she could not relax while he sat beside her. To her relief, Sir Martyn moved away at the interval and a number of Mrs Langridge's acquaintances descended, leaving Amelia free to stroll about the rooms with the earl.

'How could he sit down next to me!' she exclaimed in an undervoice. 'He has quite cut up my peace. I was in a quake lest he should begin to ask me questions.'

'No, how should that be? What could he ask you, after all? You had no need to answer him.'

She gave him a smouldering look.

'You might enjoy these cat and mouse games, sir, but I find it most uncomfortable.'

He grinned down at her.

'Poor child. I was watching you and thought you responded admirably.'

'I said nothing.'

'Quite, so he has learned nothing. My biggest concern is that he should think there is some connection between us.'

'If he should learn of Miss Templecombe!'

'Unlikely, but in any case it is time Lady Isabelle was moved. I am sorry we did not think about it sooner, but Isabelle is so settled at Midford that Delham and I have allowed the matter to rest. I shall talk to Delham about it tonight and we must find another safe haven for her.' He saw her concern and patted her hand. 'Be brave, my dear. I think we are nearing the end of the game now, and Sir Martyn's presence here only strengthens that belief.'

'Can you – will you not tell me what you are about and why you are so bent on his destruction?'

He gave her a wry smile.

'It is an old story, child, and not an edifying one. As to my plans – to know them might put you in danger.' He broke off, his smile widening as he saw Sir Martyn before them.

'Ah, Pudsey. Delightful concert, don't you think?'

Sir Martyn's smile did not reach his eyes, which remained wary.

'It is proving a very interesting evening, certainly.'

His malevolent glance flickered over Amelia.

'Do you know, Rossleigh, I believe you have been trying to mislead me?'

The earl's brows rose.

'Mislead you, sir? How can that be? Why, I have not said above a dozen words to you tonight.'

Sir Martyn's hard eyes narrowed.

'Your cleverness may let you down this time, Rossleigh. If the lady would take a word of advice,' – he glanced at Amelia – 'you would be as well to distance yourself from Lord Rossleigh, ma'am. His history will not bear close scrutiny!'

With a short bow he turned and strode away.

'What did he mean, my lord?'

The earl was smiling again.

'Pudsey? A mere nothing, madam. He is like a cornered rat, trying to make trouble. Let me escort you back to your mama.'

Sir Martyn did not return to the concert hall, and although Lord Rossleigh's attentions for the remainder of the evening were assiduous, Amelia felt he had put himself behind a barrier and would not talk to her.

The earl's distant attitude affected her as much as Sir Martyn's veiled threats and after a sleepless night she ordered her carriage and drove to Bath, on the pretext of purchasing more black gloves. The carriage pulled into the yard of the White Hart where her enquiries elicited the information that Lord Rossleigh and Lord Delham had gone out of town and were not expected back until the evening.

Lady Langridge was disappointed but not surprised. During the journey she had realized that the earl was unlikely to be found at the inn. She gave instructions to her coachman to be ready to carry her to Midford within the hour and sallied forth with her maid to Milsom Street. Since her pretext for coming to Bath was to shop she dutifully made her purchases and was about to go back to the inn when she spotted a dainty figure in a royal blue pelisse and bonnet entering a milliner's shop a few yards ahead of her. Amelia hesitated only briefly before following, and she found Mrs Strickland and her daughter demanding to try on a number of bonnets from the window. When she saw Amelia, Camilla's beautiful face registered surprise, quickly followed by such a guilty look that Lady Langridge did not doubt there was mischief afoot. She smiled pleasantly.

'Good day to you Mrs Strickland, Camilla. I did not expect to see you in Bath.'

Mrs Strickland waved one gloved hand.

'Amelia, my dear child! But we must call you *my lady* now, is that not so? How do you go on, my poor child? We had not planned to come to Bath, or we should have written to you – not that we would impose upon you and your mama at such a sad, sad time.'

'Thank you, ma'am. Where do you stay, with Camilla's grandmama?'

'Heavens no! We are at the Bull, in Stall Street,' replied Camilla.

'Oh, was there nothing suitable at the White Hart?'

Mrs Strickland hesitated, but Camilla's attention had wandered to a bonnet that the milliner was holding out to her, a high-crowned lilac silk creation with a heavy veil more suited to a dowager, Amelia thought.

'Yes, I'll take that one. What was that, Amelia? There was very likely room at the White Hart, but Sir Martyn is staying at the Bull.'

'Camilla my love, we have such a lot of purchases to make today, I think we should be going. . . .'

Mrs Strickland cut short her daughter's protests, chattering nervously as she waited impatiently for the milliner to pack the lilac bonnet that Camilla insisted she must have.

'Pray give my regards to your mama, my dear Amelia — la, I keep forgetting I should be calling you Lady Langridge, now you are a baroness. Camilla are you ready now? Come, child, say goodbye to Amelia and let us be off!'

Mrs Strickland hurried her daughter out of the shop, leaving Amelia to make her way back along Milsom Street, pondering on the lady's odd behaviour. She had said they had not planned to come to Bath, so what had brought them? Miss Stickland's artless chatter indicated that they had followed Sir Martyn, but to what purpose, she wondered. Sir Martyn could not offer Camilla marriage, and any other proposal was unthinkable. But as her coach rumbled out of Bath on its way to Midford, Amelia considered the matter more deeply and realized that Mrs Strickland was thinking of it. Her hopes of a splendid match for Camilla had not borne fruit and she probably saw Sir Martyn now as Camilla's only hope of catching a fortune.

'But at such a cost!' she exclaimed aloud. 'Foolish woman.'

Her maid, sitting opposite her in the carriage, looked at her mistress in apprehension and Amelia hastily begged pardon and reassured her that she had merely been thinking aloud.

Amelia wondered if she should ask her mother to speak to Mrs Strickland, to dissuade her from a course of action so ruinous to Camilla, but she knew the difficulty would be to make her mama believe that Mrs Strickland could contemplate allowing her daughter to become Sir Martyn's mistress. She wondered if Lord Rossleigh might help her and this brought her back to her reasons for wanting to talk to him. Unconsciously she clasped her hands together in her lap. She knew it was nonsensical, but she felt that if only she could meet with the earl, he could make everything right.

As the coach drew up at Miss Templecombe's cottage, Amelia pushed aside such thoughts: it certainly would not do to worry Lady Isabelle with such tales of her husband. Learning from the maid that Mr Lyddon was with the ladies in the sitting-room, Amelia told her that she would announce herself. She walked in to be greeted by an anguished cry from Lady Isabelle.

'Oh my lady, we are undone!'

Chapter Nineteen

Lady Isabelle cast herself into her arms and Amelia took in the scene before her. Mr Lyddon was lying on the sofa, his coat discarded and a damp cloth pressed to one eye while Miss Templecombe knelt beside him, bathing a nasty cut on his forehead.

'What in heaven's name has occurred?'

Miss Templecombe turned a pale face towards her visitor.

'Th-there was a man skulking in the garden. Mr Lyddon tried to apprehend him and — and they fought.'

'It was one of Martyn's men, I am sure of it.' muttered Lady Isabelle, her voice trembling.

Mr Lyddon tried to sit up.

'The fellow was spying at the window. I tried to catch him but he was too strong for me — knocked me out cold.'

'Hush, sir, lie back now and rest. You did what you could.'

Lady Isabelle had been crying on Amelia's shoulder but now she raised her head.

'But don't you see? He will go to my husband. I am lost!'

When was this?' asked Amelia, thinking quickly. 'When did this man make off?'

Miss Templecombe looked at the clock.

'About an hour since.'

'Then there is no time to lose. We must get Lady Isabelle away from here.'

'But where?' demanded Miss Templecombe. 'If Sir Martyn has learned of your connection, Amelia, then Langridge Court will not be safe.'

'Oh if only Henry were here to help me,' sobbed Isabelle.

'I am sorry to say that Lord Rossleigh and your brother are gone out of town and are not expected back before evening.' Amelia looked across at Mr Lyddon. 'You once told me, sir, that if you had your way you would take Lady Isabelle abroad.'

'Well yes, but—'

'Then I think that is what you must do. I will take Lady Isabelle and Miss T. to the Court with me, and you must ride to Bath to leave a message for Lord Delham and to collect your things. . . .'

Miss Templecombe shook her head at that.

'My dear, I am afraid the gentleman will not be able to ride anywhere for some hours yet. He can hardly stand.'

'She's right,' agreed Mr Lyddon. 'I feel as weak as a kitten.'

Amelia bit her lip, frowning.

'Is there anything in Bath that you must have?'

'No, a few clothes, that is all.'

'Then you must buy everything you need on the road.' She turned to the ladies. 'Quickly now, ask Betty to help you pack. My carriage is outside and will carry you all to Langridge Court. You must go too, Miss T. I fear if Sir Martyn comes here and fmds his quarry flown he will be very dangerous.'

Miss Templecombe nodded absently.

'But your coach will not hold us all, love. Betty or your maid must stay behind.'

A faint, mischievous smile touched Amelia's lips.

'No, you will all go. I intend to take Mr Lyddon's horse and ride to Bath to alert Lord Delham. Does anyone in the village own a lady's saddle, Miss T?'

'Well, yes, the vicar's wife has one — it is already in the

barn where Mr Lyddon stables his horse.'

'Good. Let us hope it will fit! Very well, what next? Isabelle, you should go and pack. Miss T. do you have paper and ink? I should write a short note to Mama for you to carry for me.' While the ladies hurried out of the room to pack their bags Amelia swiftly scribbled her letter. 'I have a little money on me that I will give to Lady Isabelle and I shall ask Mama to give you the purse from the estate office, Mr Lyddon. It should be sufficient to get you across the Channel – after that you will have to manage as best you can until Lord Delham can reach you.'

Mr Lyddon sat up, gingerly feeling his jaw.

'Thank you, ma'am, but I have some money of my own.'

'Then take that as well.' The baroness smiled. 'I have never before participated in an elopement but I have always thought it would be a costly business.'

Mr Lyddon gave a weak laugh.

'Aye, you may be right. But I cannot let you ride off alone.'

'You have only one horse, sir, and you are not capable of riding it. The sooner Lord Delham knows of the situation the better. Where will you sail from?'

'I hadn't thought . . . Bristol would be most obvious, and the first place Pudsey will look! We'll head south, Plymouth perhaps and cross to France from there. Yes, Plymouth – I have friends there. Don't worry, my lady. I'll take care of Isabelle.'

'I am sure you will, sir.'

A few minutes later the ladies returned, dressed for travelling and with their belongings hastily crammed into several portmanteaux. Amelia handed over the letter for her mother, gave brief instructions to the coachman and stood back to watch the carriage roll away. She felt strangely elated by the events of the afternoon, conscious that the inactivity of the past two months had left her with a surplus of energy

needing an outlet. Carefully she shut up the house and made
her way to the barn to find Mr Lyddon's horse. She had hoped
there would be a village boy or farm hand to help her to
change the saddle, but the barn was deserted and the whole
village slumbered peacefully under the scorching summer
sun.

It took Amelia some time to locate the lady's saddle, which
was hidden behind a pile of grain sacks. More minutes
passed as she dusted it off and carried it over to the grey
gelding, who eyed it nervously. By the time she had saddled
up, Lady Langridge's black gown was woefully dusty. She
brushed it as best she could, uttering up thanks that she had
her veil to disguise her identity when she rode into Bath. She
made a last check of the girths, untied the reins and was
about to lead the horse to a mounting block when a shadow
fell across the open door.

'So, madam, you think to meddle in my plans.'

'Sir Martyn! I-I do not understand you, sir.'

'Don't act the innocent with me, madam. You've been
hiding my wife here.'

'I have done nothing of the kind.'

'You are a poor liar, Lady Langridge. Where have they gone
now?'

She stared at him defiantly, holding her breath as he
stepped forward to stand directly before her. She wondered if
she could push past him, but a quick glance showed her that
his weasel-faced groom was blocking the doorway.

'I'd wager Rossleigh has a hand in this.'

'No, he—' She stopped, realizing her mistake.

'Oh?' He took her chin in his large hand, forcing her to look
up at him. 'Hmm, pretty enough. I can see Rossleigh might
find you entertaining, for a while.' He smiled at the sight of
her flushed cheeks. 'You think I should be beating you to find
out where my wife might be? I have my spies out searching,

they will find her. In the meantime I am more interested in putting an end to Rossleigh's little intrigues.' He reached out and pulled a piece of cord from one of the empty sacks. 'Give me your hands.'

'No!'

A struggle ensued but it was an unequal one, and he bound her hands tightly before her. 'If you try to run I shall tie your ankles too.'

She glared at him, maintaining her silence as he threw her up on to the saddle. Her face flamed as Sir Martyn pushed her boots into the stirrups and straightened her gown, his hands lingering on her ankle, then moving slowly up towards her knee. He laughed as he felt her shudder.

'Don't worry, I'm not going to touch you — yet. But I warn you, do not try to run away or to scream. I'd take great pleasure in putting some bruises on that slender throat of yours. Hold on!'

Chapter Twenty

*A*lthough the afternoon was well advanced it was still hot on the road. Two riders cantered across the open meadow and up to the tree-lined ridge, where they slowed to a walking pace to rest the horses.

'Well, that went better than I hoped.' Lord Delham stopped to take out his handkerchief and mop his brow.

Lord Rossleigh pulled up beside him.

'Yes. I thought Jameson would offer more objections to our taking the woman away.'

'He certainly didn't want to be troubled with the magistrate. What do you think Pudsey will do when he finds she's gone?'

'I don't know, but that may not be for some time. Jameson did not appear to know that Pudsey is in Bath, so any message will be sent to London.'

'And you think she will be safe?'

The earl nodded.

'The house we have hired is very isolated, and as you saw I have two good men to act as guards. Poor creature, she is very confused, but the couple I have engaged to look after her have lived on my Banbury estate for many years and I trust them to treat her with kindness. I wish we could have moved sooner, but I had to ensure that I had a safe house and trustworthy people to care for her. The doctor will call on her

179

tomorrow morning, and once I have all the evidence we will act.'

'And Issy will be free.' Lord Delham sighed. 'Ross, thank you—'

'Save your gratitude, whelp, until the trick is finally won. Besides, you know I have done this as much for my sake as yours.'

'Ay, to lay an old ghost.' Lord Delham held out his hand. 'Well done, my friend.' He looked up. 'We are but a few miles from Midford – would you object if I left you here and slipped down to see Isabelle? I will say nothing to her of our venture, I promise.'

'I believe you, Henry. Go on, and give her my regards.'

With a loud halloo and a wave of his crop Lord Delham set his horse cantering away. Lord Rossleigh watching him, smiling, then turned his own mount towards Bath. He had only travelled a mile or so when the trees on the ridge grew thinner, giving him a clear view of the valley road below. A slight movement caught his eye and he stopped to get a better view. There were three horses, the first was a big roan hunter carrying a large rider in a dark-red coat. The earl nodded slowly: it was almost certainly Sir Martyn. He was followed by a smaller man – a groom, possibly, riding a few paces behind, but riding close beside Sir Martyn was another figure, a lady, dressed from head to toe in black.

Lady Langridge shifted in the saddle, trying to ease her tense muscles. She felt stiff, as though she had been riding for hours, but the sun was only a little lower in the sky.

'Where are you taking me?'

Sir Martyn looked around briefly, his face shiny with sweat beneath the brim of his hat. 'To the west, into the setting sun.'

'Not to Bath, then.'

'Good God no. How could I expect to keep you there? No, we go to Keynsham. There is a house there where I can leave you and it will make no odds if you protest or accuse me of kidnap, you will not be believed – they hold many such deranged creatures.'

Despite the sun, Amelia shivered.

'You would lock me in a mad-house?'

Sir Martyn shrugged.

'Those who interfere with my plans must be punished.'

'It is you who are mad!'

'No, how can that be? Think of the logic, ma'am. Where else can I hold you safe from harm, yet protect myself from your accusations? In a year or two the world will have forgotten you. Be thankful it is a private asylum. If it were Bedlam the gentry would be paying to laugh at your torment.'

'But I have family. They will not permit this.'

'True, but first they have to find you. And don't expect Rossleigh to come to your aid: I had thought when I followed him to Bath that he had learned something, but it was you that brought him here, for you had hidden my wife with your old governess.'

Amelia felt sick with fear, but she tried to hide it, determined to keep alert for a means of escape. They dropped into a valley and the lengthening shadows merged into a deeper gloom as they followed the path into a wood. They stopped at a stream and Sir Martyn dismounted, handing the reins of his own horse and Amelia's to his groom. Tearing off his hat and wig he dropped to his knees and began to splash his face with the cool water.

'Will you not untie me, sir, that I may do the same?'

He laughed coarsely. 'Do you take me for a fool?'

'Well, yes, as a matter of fact,' came a voice from the shadows.

With an oath Sir Martyn jumped to his feet, looking

around in time to see Lord Rossleigh emerge from the trees, a pistol glinting in one hand.

'Release the lady.'

'To you, sir? I think not.' Sir Martyn raised one hand and clicked his fingers. 'You have your pistol aimed at my heart, Rossleigh, but you will see that Catling is also armed, and he has orders to shoot the lady rather than release her. I, too, would do the same, so make your choice: you can shoot me, or him, but either way the lady dies.' His evil smile grew as he watched the earl. 'Just so, my lord. Now perhaps you would like to put down your weapon.'

'No!' Amelia's stifled cry went unnoticed. The earl looked up at the groom, who was levelling a horse-pistol at Amelia.

'You need not doubt he will shoot, Rossleigh,' sneered Sir Martyn. 'It would not be the first time he has killed for me.'

With a faint shrug, the earl lowered his arm and stooped to put the weapon on the ground. Sir Martyn reached to his belt.

'Very wise, my lord. What a happy coincidence that you have shown up. I have no doubt the lady was hoping you might rescue her, like some latter-day knight, but now you are here it allows me to disillusion her, to tell her that you are not the shining hero she thinks you.' Sir Martyn levelled his own pistol at the earl. 'Of course, she would never believe my word, but you will tell her, Rossleigh. Tell her that you are no better than a common murderer.'

'You may rot in hell, Pudsey!'

'Very possibly, but you will be there with me — in fact, you have been there already, have you not, for the past twelve years, since you killed your sister! Oh, do I hear you protest, Lady Langridge? Do you not want to believe your hero is so flawed?'

Amelia gave a scornful laugh.

'You lie, sir. It cannot be true.'

'No?' purred Sir Martyn, his evil smile fixed upon the earl. 'Well, Rossleigh, will you deny it?'

The earl returned the stare, his face pale.

'You know I will not.'

'There, my lady,' cried Sir Martyn, turning to look at her in triumph. 'What think you of the great Lord Rossleigh now, eh?'

Amelia saw her chance: the groom's attention was fixed on the two men by the stream, and as Sir Martyn laughed up at her she took a deep breath and hurled herself out of her saddle. The groom was so close that she knocked him from his horse, the pistol flying from his hand as they crashed to the ground. At the same moment the earl launched himself at Sir Martyn. There was a loud retort that sent the horses careering away into the trees. Collecting her wits, Amelia rolled over to pick up the groom's pistol. She lifted the weapon between her tied hands and pointed it at the servant, who scrambled up and took to his heels after the horses. Breathing heavily, she turned back to see Sir Martyn and the earl still grappling. She dare not fire the pistol while they were locked together, but even as she watched, the earl tripped Sir Martyn, who fell heavily and lay still, Lord Rossleigh on his knees beside him. Amelia ran forward.

'Quickly, my lord, get up, let us go.'

Lord Rossleigh rose unsteadily to his feet and she saw the red stain spreading over his left sleeve.

'We must go, sir. Now!'

'My horse is tethered in the bushes — but first, give me the pistol.'

He dropped it into his pocket then began to untie her. Amelia shifted restlessly as he struggled with the knots but at last she was free and she took his arm.

'Come now, let us go.'

She led him into the bushes where Trojan was waiting

patiently. Lord Rossleigh staggered and Amelia grabbed at his coat, holding him up.

'Another yard, sir, and you are there.' She pushed him toward the horse, where he clung to the saddle, barely conscious. 'Quickly, my lord, mount, mount!'

Straining, she helped him up into the saddle while behind her she heard Sir Martyn calling to his groom. She looked up. Lord Rossleigh was slumped over the horse's neck. In desperation she pulled up her skirts, put one foot into the stirrup and hauled herself up behind the earl to sit astride the horse. She put her arms about the earl, took the reins and drove her heels into the horse's flanks. Not a moment too soon the horse trotted away, for she heard someone crashing through the bushes behind them and the blast of a pistol shot made her flinch. She kicked the hunter to a canter and did not allow the pace to slacken until they were clear of the trees and had left the valley behind them. Then Trojan slowed to a walk, but still Amelia pressed on until they reached a small copse. Once in the shelter of the trees she reined in the hunter and looked back. The open ground they had covered was empty, with no sign of pursuit and she uttered up a silent prayer. Lord Rossleigh was only semi-conscious and it took all her strength to stop him slipping out of the saddle. Moving on again, she doubled back through the trees, heading on to the downs, all the time watching for riders behind them. The sun had almost set and she knew that in the gathering dusk it would be impossible to find their way. The great black horse stumbled and she murmured encouragement, her arms aching from holding the earl before her. When they came across a barn in the lee of the hill she drew rein, listening. There were the faint sounds of running water nearby and she could just make out a small stream cascading down on the far side of the barn.

'We will stop here. Hold on, sir, I am going to dismount.'

184

Dropping to the ground Amelia led the hunter through the narrow door. The earl was slumped over his neck and just slipped under the door frame. The barn was not large and the big horse took up more than half the space.

'Come sir, there is straw here for you, and a sack of turnips for a pillow.'

To her intense relief she heard him chuckle.

'What more could we wish for?'

Fighting back her tears she helped the earl alight and half-carried him to the far corner of the barn, where he lay back against the turnip sacks, breathing raggedly. Amelia gently eased the coat from his shoulders. He bit his lip, holding back a cry of pain, but as she pulled the sleeve from his left arm he lapsed into unconsciousness. Quickly Amelia struggled to free him of the coat and regarded with dismay the blood-soaked sleeve of his shirt. There was blood too on his waistcoat, but she decided it would subject the earl to too much discomfort to remove it. Screwing up her courage she ripped away the shirt sleeve and tore off some of her petticoat to wipe away the blood until she could see the actual wound. There was a deep gash, just below the shoulder and she gave a sigh of relief as she realized the bullet had passed through the flesh. While the earl was unconscious she removed the remains of her petticoat and proceeded to tear it into strips to bandage the arm, anxious to do as much as possible before the darkness closed in. She bound the wound tightly to stop the sluggish bleeding then got up to explore their shelter. There was no lantern, but she found an old pan which she filled with water from the stream. Then, in the last of the light, she unsaddled Trojan and used handfuls of straw to rub him down.

She had just finished when the earl stirred. She dusted her hands and went to kneel beside him, holding the pan to his lips.

'Be easy, sir,' she whispered, as he turned his head rest-lessly. 'Drink. It is merely water.'

He paused. 'Amelia?'

Tenderly she pushed a lock of hair from his brow. 'Yes, my lord.'

'Where the devil are we?'

'I have no idea, but I don't think we were followed.'

He lifted his hand until his fingers were touching her face. 'Foolish girl. You could have been killed.'

She put her hand over his.

'So too could you. You risked your life for me.'

His hand crept around her neck and he pulled her against him.

'Thank God you are safe.'

'Pray God you suffer no lasting hurt, sir.'

He sighed. 'It hurts like the devil.'

'I think it is only a flesh wound. Shall I try to make you more comfortable?'

His arm tightened about her.

'I am comfortable. Lay your head on me, Amelia. You too need to sleep.'

With a tiny sigh she relaxed against him, listening to the thud of his heart through his embroidered waistcoat. As the last shreds of light faded into darkness, they slept.

Chapter Twenty One

*A*melia opened her eyes and wondered where she could be. As she became aware of the gentle rise and fall of a chest beneath her cheek, memory returned. She lay still, savouring the peace of the moment, knowing it could not last. Eventually she raised her head and stared into the earl's sleeping face. He looked pale, and a dark stubble shadowed his chin and his cheeks. As she watched, the lids fluttered and his blue eyes looked back at her.

'Good morning, my lady.'

'Good day to you, my lord.' She went to rise, but his good arm tightened around her

'No, stay a little. It is early yet.'

She relaxed again, revelling in the comfort of his arm about her.

'Sir, what if – what if Sir Martyn is still looking for us?'

'Then we shall have to outrun him. We cannot be far from Bath; he would not dare to harm us there.'

Amelia screwed up her courage.

'Sir?'

'Yes?'

'He — he said . . . your sister.'

There was silence. Amelia swallowed and risked a peep at the earl. His face was grim.

'Will you tell me? I thought — Lady Charlotte. . . .'

'I had another sister, once.' He let her go and pushed

himself into a sitting position. 'It was more than a dozen years ago. I had just attained my majority when my sister Susannah eloped. She was heiress to a considerable fortune, but the man she had chosen was a rogue.'

'Sir Martyn?'

'Ay, the very same! My parents had forbidden the marriage, but my father was bedridden, so I took it upon myself to go after them.'

Amelia sat very still, watching the play of emotion on his face.

'I caught up with them before the marriage could take place. They were at an inn at Grantham. I ordered Susannah return with me. She refused. I had brought pistols and swords and demanded that the blackguard fight me in a duel. Susannah begged me to desist – begged us both, for her sake, not to fight, but we were both hot for blood. We chose swords and fought immediately, there at the inn. Irregular, I know, but we were neither of us for waiting. Susannah was distraught but we ignored her. I was in the grip of a blind rage, I would have blood, fool that I was.' He paused, and it seemed to Amelia that he was looking back over the years, something of the boy's anger reflected in his face. He sighed. 'We fought, but he was older than I, a master of the duello and I – well, I was nothing but a callow boy. He toyed with me, pinked me neatly and could have killed me at any time. He may well have meant to do so but Susannah, who had been watching from the corner of the room, picked up one of my pistols, put it to her breast . . . She died immediately. It seems she could not bear to leave her lover, nor could she face the heartbreak of her family.'

Amelia put her hand to her mouth, blinking rapidly.

'You poor boy.'

He smiled, the self-mockery in his eyes cutting her like a knife.

'Oh, I had succeeded in my aim, I had foiled the elopement. My father died soon after, his heart broken, and I vowed revenge. I went abroad, studied duelling with the finest swordsmen in Italy until I too was a master, but by the time I came back to England the man had married again, this time the sister of my best friend.'

'Lady Isabelle.'

'The very same.' He closed his eyes. 'My greatest regret is that I kept Susannah's elopement a secret from Henry Delham. The matter was hushed up you see; after all, it reflected credit on no one. But if I had told him, had not allowed my stupid pride to keep me silent!'

'But – forgive me – twelve years ago Lord Delham must have been a schoolboy.'

'Ay, but our families had always been friends, if we had taken them into our confidence, perhaps Isabelle would have been safe. By the time I returned to England it was too late. Issy was married and so in love that I could not, would not do anything to hurt her. Pudsey flaunted his conquest before me and, as his true nature asserted itself; she began to suffer. Henry begged her to leave him, but she would have none of it, preferring to think herself in love with him. The rest you know. All these years I have been looking for the perfect revenge and now I think I have found it.' He looked at her, and she was relieved to see something of the old gleam back in his eyes. 'Pray, madam, do not question me further on this. Delham and I have to put together the final pieces, then we will spring the trap. Tell me instead how you came to be with Pudsey.'

'I fear it will not please you, my lord.'

'Tell me.'

She settled back in the corner, her hands clasped lightly before her.

'I called at Midford yesterday to find the house in uproar. One of Sir Martyn's spies had discovered them. Mr Lyddon tried to detain him but failed, and was injured in the process. I gave them my carriage – they were to leave Miss Templecombe and her servant at Langridge Court and Mr Lyddon,' – here Amelia's confidence faltered – 'Mr Lyddon is taking Lady Isabelle out of the country.'

'The devil he is! And whose idea was this?'

She forced herself to meet his gaze.

'It was mine, sir. I had been told at the White Hart that you and Lord Delham were not expected back before nightfall and it was vital to remove Isabelle with all speed.'

'So you sent her off with a penniless gambler.'

She raised her chin.

'You and Lord Delham had failed to find her an alternative hiding place. I gave instructions for Mr Lyddon to be given money from my estate fund – and if he loves her, which I believe he does – that makes him the most suitable person to take care of her. He was taking her to the coast, preferring to cross from Devon into France than to risk Sir Martyn catching up with them at Bristol. They promised to send word of their direction as soon as they were safe.'

She saw his brow darken and thought for a moment he would swear at her, but he bit back any retort, merely shaking his head.

'Henry left me yesterday to call upon Issy.'

'He will be concerned, then, if he found the house empty. Let us hope he has returned to Bath and we can give him the true story as soon as we get back.' She went to rise but he put out his good hand to prevent her.

'Not yet, madam, you have not finished your tale. Why did you not go to Langridge Court with everyone else?'

'Mr Lyddon was not well enough to ride to Bath to leave word for Lord Delham, so I elected to do so, there being no room in the carriage for all of us. Unfortunately Sir Martyn found me.' She frowned. 'I think – it seemed to me that he did not wish to find Isabelle, but was more interested in punishing *you*, my lord. He – he told me he was taking me to an – an asylum in Keynsham, where I could be incarcerated without hope of being found.' She paused, shivering. 'That is why I was not afraid to fight for my freedom, sir. I would rather die than enter such a place.'

He stared at her, then reached forward to put his fingers on her cheek.

'He does not know that Delham and I have already discovered this hiding place of his, but even so, if he had harmed you. . . .'

She blinked rapidly, putting her head on one side to trap his hand.

'But he did not, sir.' She closed her eyes for a moment, savouring the touch of his palm on her cheek, then with sudden resolution she got to her feet, determined to be practical. 'Now, my lord, do you think you can ride?'

The earl glanced down at the bloody bandage around his arm.

'I think so, if you would bind it up again?'

'Of course.'

She quickly pulled off another petticoat, discarding the lacy flounce, and began to tear the cotton into strips. The earl watched her, smiling.

'What a resourceful woman you are, Lady Langridge.'

'Because I can bandage a wound? Most women can do as much.'

'But you also carried me off safe when Sir Martyn was determined to kill me.' He frowned. 'I cannot remember much of that – how did we get here with only one horse?'

'I climbed up behind you and rode astride.' She lowered her gaze, conscious of her burning cheeks. 'Thank goodness it was growing dark, for I fear there was more than my garters on display!'

191

'I wish I had seen it.'

The blush deepened but she ignored his words and began to remove the blood-soaked bandages.

'Thank heaven the bleeding has stopped. I will bind it up as best I may and that must do until we can get to Bath, and a surgeon.'

'I need no sawbones pulling me about. Only get me back to the White Hart and my man O'Brien will do the rest.'

'At least let me make a sling for you, my lord. Your coat I fear is ruined.' She held it up to show him that one side was caked with black, dried blood.

'We will leave it here. I never cared much for the cut, after all. I will make the journey in my waistcoat, if you do not object, madam.'

She met his glance, her eyes reflecting the twinkle in his own.

'Thankfully your taste in waistcoats is impeccable, my lord.'

'Thank you. Let us get on then.'

Using his good hand the earl helped Amelia to saddle Trojan before leading him out into the early morning sunlight.

'Let me mount first, and I'll lift you up before me. Early as it is, we will need to be a little more circumspect, riding into the city.'

Once he was in the saddle, Lord Rossleigh hauled Amelia up until she was sitting across the saddle before him, cradled in his good arm, which also held the reins. Conscious of his body so close to her own, Amelia felt her cheeks redden and she tried to remain stiffly upright.

'Relax a little, my lady.' His breath was warm on her cheek. 'We will both travel more comfortably if you lean against me.'

Once they reached the road it took the earl a very short time to find the route into Bath. It was still early when they rode into the city and there were only servants and the occasional hawker abroad to note their arrival. They rode immediately to the White Hart where Lord Rossleigh ushered Amelia into his private parlour, a large room with two deep bay windows looking out on to the inn-yard.

'Most of the city still sleeps. Would you like me to order a carriage to take you home? I will bring the magistrate to you later for you to make your complaint against Sir Martyn.'

'And what will you do, sir?'

'I am going to change into fresh clothes, get my man to shave me, then Delham and I will close the net on Pudsey — as we had planned.'

She took a deep breath.

'Could — could I stay? Once I return to the Court Mama will insist that I remain there. Having been a part of this adventure I too want to see you catch this villain. Please let me stay.'

Before he could answer a hasty step was heard in the passage and Lord Delham burst in. He was wearing only his shirt and breeches, and his wig was askew as if he had clapped it on his head in haste.

'Ross! Where the devil have you been — I have been in a frenzy all night—' he broke off as his eyes fell upon Amelia, and he hesitated in the doorway. 'My lady! I — Ross, your arm — what in heaven's name—?'

'Good morning Henry, you have come to tell me that you rode to Midford yesterday and found Issy gone, is that not so? Well, I think I can allay some of your fears on that matter, at least.'

'Yes, well, thank you, but—'

Lord Rossleigh took his arm.

'Come upstairs with me and I will tell you the whole while O'Brien makes me presentable.'

Amelia stepped forward.

'My lord — may I stay?'

The smile he gave her made her spirits soar.

'Lady,' he said at last, 'how can I refuse you, when you have saved my life? I will order you a room, and we must send word to Mrs Langridge to tell her you are safe. And I suggest we ask the landlady to do what she can to clean your gown. I will tell the landlord to set breakfast in here in about — what — an hour? Will that suit you?'

A little over an hour later, Lady Amelia descended to the private parlour, looking much refreshed. A chambermaid had provided a comb and pins for her hair and her black crepe gown had been brushed to remove the worst of the dirt. She entered the room to find the earl and Lord Delham discussing a hearty breakfast.

'Ah, Lady Langridge!' Lord Delham jumped up and stepped forward to escort her to a chair. 'Ross has been telling me of your adventures yesterday. I must say my peace was quite cut up when I found the house at Midford all shut up, but Ross tells me they were discovered by one of Pudsey's men.'

'Yes, my lord. He was spotted but managed to get away to tell Sir Martyn. It — it seemed advisable to remove Lady Isabelle immediately.'

'Hmm, she's gone off with that fellow Lyddon, Ross tells me.'

'Yes, my lord. He is taking her abroad.'

Silently she poured herself a cup of coffee while Lord Delham frowned over her words. At length the young man gave a resigned sigh.

'Well, if she's happy with him, it is probably for the best. At least until we have finished with Pudsey.'

Amelia looked from one gentleman to the other.

'What are you going to do?'

'Confront him,' said the earl.

'But — will he see you?'

Lord Rossleigh smiled, a dangerous glitter in his eyes.

'Oh yes. I have sent a message to him at the Bull, requesting him to call here at two o'clock this afternoon.' He refilled his coffee cup. 'That does not give us much time. Henry, you know what to do. Take my coach, I have hired a couple of outriders to accompany you and they are armed, too, in case you need them.'

'Oh I don't expect any trouble,' replied Lord Delham. 'When I called at the Bull earlier this morning – just before you returned here, in fact – the boots told me that Pudsey came in late last night, angry as a bear and explaining his bruised face by saying he had been thrown by his horse.'

Lady Langridge stared at him admiringly.

'You have been abroad already this morning, my lord? I applaud your diligence.'

The young man flushed.

'Yes, well, with Issy flown and Ross missing overnight, I couldn't sleep, and had to do what I could to gather information. When Ross told me this morning how he had come upon you, I could hardly believe it. Thank God he found you when he did. We had come from the asylum earlier that day, and my blood runs cold to think of what might have happened to you.'

'Yes, and it is unkind of you to remind the lady of it, Henry. Now if you have finished your breakfast, my carriage is ordered and I'll thank you not to keep my horses standing. Get back here as soon as you can, my friend.'

With a final, cheerful word Lord Delham departed, leaving Amelia alone with the earl.

'You will find paper, pens and ink on the table in the corner, ma'am. If you would like to write a brief note to your mama I will have my groom take it immediately to Langridge Court. Of if you prefer, I will have a carriage ordered. You could be home within the hour.'

'No, I want to stay.'

'Very well. I have already sent a note to the magistrate, asking him to attend me. You can tell him your story when he comes. It is yet another charge against Sir Martyn.'

'Thank you.' She rose. 'I wonder, sir, if I might trouble you a little further: the chambermaid has offered to go out and buy me some petticoats, but I gave my purse to Lady Isabelle yesterday. . . .'

'Of course, ma'am. Since you gave up your petticoats for me, it is only reasonable that I should replace them.'

'Oh no, no, I did not mean that at all, I was only too glad to be able to help you. Of course I shall repay you.'

He laughed. 'Pray don't become missish with me, my lady.' He held out his purse. 'It will not be the first time I have purchased underwear for a lady.'

Blushing to the roots of her hair, Amelia took the purse and fled from the room.

It was some time past noon when Lady Langridge left her room again, her new petticoats in place and her hair neatly curled and pinned up. She found Lord Rossleigh alone in the parlour where the table had been cleared of breakfast dishes and was now covered with papers. Lord Rossleigh was seated at the table, frowning over pages of neat black writing. His left arm rested in a fresh sling and she noticed that he had put on a new shirt and waistcoat plus a clean pair of buckskins, and his man had cleaned and polished his top boots until they shone and only close inspection would reveal the deep scratches in the leather. He looked up as she came in.

'I am sorry, my lord. Do I disturb you?'

'Not at all, come in. Shall I call for coffee?'

'No, thank you. When will the magistrate be here? Will I be

obliged to tell him the whole story, I mean, about Lady Isabelle?'

'I think it would be as well. Sir Jonas Tavistock is Justice of the Peace here and I would not have him think we are keeping anything from him. I have had word that he will call here at one o'clock.'

'And what are those papers?'

'Statements and depositions that will, I hope, convict Pudsey.'

She came to the table and lifted one paper, then another.

'And you will be revenged.'

He did not answer immediately.

'I have worked towards this moment for over a decade.' He sighed and sat back. 'But if truth were told that does not seem so important now. Oh, I want Pudsey brought to justice, but more than that I want the whole episode finished. My sister is dead, nothing can bring her back. It is time I put this behind me and made a new life for myself.'

'I am glad, my lord.'

There was a light scratching on the door and the landlord looked in.

'Sir Jonas is here for you, Lord Rossleigh.'

'Send him in.'

Sir Jonas was an elderly gentleman, dressed in a brown velvet frock-coat and a plain silk waistcoat that strained over his ample stomach. He had sleepy blue eyes and an edge to his voice that suggested he was not best pleased at being summoned to the inn. However, when Lord Rossleigh explained the reason for his presence, the eyes grew keener, and Sir Jonas took a seat by the table, clasping his hands together.

'A foiled kidnapping, you say? Very well, madam, perhaps you will tell me exactly what occurred?'

Lady Langridge carefully recounted the events of the previ-

197

ous day and she found herself blushing a little when she told Sir Jonas of Lord Rossleigh's part in her rescue. She did her best to remain calm and to relate only the facts to him. When she had finished, Sir Jonas sat quietly for some minutes, steepling his fingers together while he thought over her story.

'This is a serious accusation, my lady.'

'I know it, sir.'

'And are there any witnesses to this — er — kidnap?'

'Only Catling, Sir Martyn's groom.'

'A man unlikely to speak out against his master.' He paused again. 'Tell me, madam, why did you not return immediately to your family this morning?'

Amelia glanced towards the earl.

'I-I wanted to remain in Bath until I had laid this charge against Sir Martyn.'

'But I could as easily have ridden out to Langridge Court.' He rose and took a few measured steps about the room. 'You tell me that yesterday you helped Lady Isabelle Pudsey to run away from her lawful husband, and you, my lord, accuse this same wronged husband of putting a bullet through you, and after a night spent heaven knows where, the lady elects to remain here with you when one would expect any gently born young person to return immediately to the bosom of her family.'

Amelia felt the hot colour rushing to her cheeks. She saw the earl's jaw tighten as he rose from his seat.

'Yes, it does sound incredible, Sir Jonas, but when you have heard the rest of my evidence against the man, you will see that it is all of a piece. I am even now waiting for Lord Delham — Lady Isabelle's brother, to arrive with a vital witness to Pudsey's infamy.' He looked towards one of the windows, where a carriage had drawn up outside, blocking the light from the room. 'As to restoring Lady Langridge to her family, I think that event is about to take place.'

Amelia glanced at the earl, frowning as she heard voices outside the door.

'Oh heavens;' she murmured, recognizing at least one of the voices.

'Amelia my dear — thank God.' Mrs Langridge flew across the room to her daughter. 'I have been out of my mind with worry!'

'Mama, you had my note — I told you I was safe.' Amelia hugged her. 'You should not have come here.'

'Not come! No caring parent could sit at home after reading such a note.' declared Mr Crannock, following Mrs Langridge into the parlour.

'Edmund! What are you doing here?' Amelia could not keep the note of irritation from her voice.

Mrs Langridge patted her hand.

'When you did not come home yesterday, love, Edmund kindly offered to stay with me.'

'Your mama was understandably overwrought,' put in Mr Crannock. 'And when your note arrived this morning I questioned the messenger and ascertained your direction. I must tell you, Amelia, I think it most improper that you did not return to your home at the first opportunity.'

Amelia put up her chin.

'And I will do so, as soon as my business here is finished. I have been making a deposition to Sir Jonas, who is—'

'Ah yes, no need to introduce us,' Mr Crannock interrupted her, nodding at Sir Jonas. 'But perhaps you can explain to us why it was necessary for you to stay away overnight?'

'I can, of course, but I do not see that it is anything to do with you!' declared Amelia, two angry spots of colour flaming in her cheeks.

Lord Rossleigh stepped forward.

'Lady Langridge has been involved in a kidnap.' He

paused, allowing his audience time to digest his words, then gave a brief account of events. Mrs Langridge gasped as he told her of Sir Martyn's actions, and she clung to her daughter's hand, throwing frequent glances towards her as if to assure herself that Amelia was indeed unharmed.

'Well, well, a most unfortunate time you have had of it, my dear,' remarked Mr Crannock, when the earl had finished his tale. 'But you should come back with us now, Amelia. You can do no more here.'

'On the contrary,' put in Sir Jonas, 'we are now awaiting Sir Martyn's arrival, and I mean to charge him with these accusations and see how he can account for himself.'

Amelia led her mother to a chair beside the empty fireplace and coaxed her to sit down.

'You must see, Mama, that I cannot leave yet.'

'Yes, but if Sir Martyn is the villain you paint him, Rossleigh, will be come?' asked Mr Crannock.

The earl looked down at the papers spread over the table.

'Oh yes,' he said softly, 'he will come.'

Amelia raised her head.

'But there is no reason for you to be here, Edmund, or Mama.'

Their voices were instantly raised in protest, until the earl put up his hand.

'I have no objection to them staying, if Sir Jonas is content.'

The magistrate nodded and Mr Crannock withdrew to a chair in the corner, while Mrs Langridge continued to press Amelia for more details of her ordeal. Sir Jonas took out his watch.

'It is past two o'clock, sir. I will give you another ten minutes, but then I shall take my leave of you, and issue a warrant for Sir Martyn's arrest.'

Lord Rossleigh nodded toward the window.

'No need for that, Sir Jonas. He is here now.'

A heavy tread was heard approaching, the door opened and Sir Martyn Pudsey strode in.

He glanced around the room and smiled, although his eyes remained wary. He swept off his hat and made his bow.

'Such esteemed company! I was not expecting to attend a levée, Rossleigh.'

Sir Jonas stood up.

'You are Sir Martyn Pudsey? I have to tell you, sir, that you are called upon to answer the most serious charges of kidnap and attempted murder.' Sir Martyn's brows went up as Sir Jonas continued, 'Lady Langridge accuses you of abducting her with intent to unlawfully imprison her in an asylum.'

'Oh?' His lip curled. 'And did I — er — carry off the lady in a closed carriage?'

Sir Jonas looked towards Amelia.

'No, I was on horseback.'

Sir Martyn's smile grew.

'Dear me. And when did this alleged abduction take place, in the middle of the day? Do you mean to say that I led you through the streets and you made no attempt to call for help?'

She met his mocking glance steadily.

'You know you had threatened to throttle me.'

Sir Jonas cleared his throat.

'You are also accused, sir, of wounding Lord Rossleigh, of attempting to murder him. Do you deny that?'

Sir Martyn's cold eyes flickered over the earl, noting the bandage and the sling.

'No, I do not deny it. But, Sir Jonas, let me put before you another version of events. I met with Lady Langridge yesterday for – ah—' He smiled again. 'Delicacy prevents me from putting it into words. Suffice to say that we were riding back towards Bath when we were overtaken by Lord Rossleigh in what I can only describe as a passion born of jealousy. We fought over the lady and he went off with the, ah, shall we say, the honours.'

Amelia gasped. She saw the look of horror on her mother's face and exclaimed, 'That is not true!'

'What a fertile imagination you have, Pudsey.' drawled Lord Rossleigh.

Sir Martyn touched the purple bruise on his cheek.

'Unlike you, Lord Rossleigh, I am prepared to admit that passion – or would lust be a more appropriate term? Lust made us adversaries.'

The earl's face darkened with anger but Sir Jonas raised his hand.

'I need witnesses to confirm your stories. Are there any?'

'My groom was with me,' offered Sir Martyn, 'although he could do little to help me once the lady had decided to throw in her lot with Lord Rossleigh.'

'Sir Jonas, he lies.' cried Amelia. 'It is not at all how he describes it.'

'Thank you, madam, I have heard your story, and justice demands that Sir Martyn should be free to defend himself.'

Lord Rossleigh stepped forward.

'Perhaps we should move on to the other charges I wish to bring.'

Sir Martyn walked to a chair and sat down, drawling, 'Will this take long? I have other plans for the day.'

'No, not long.'

As Lord Rossleigh sifted through the papers on the table, Amelia looked out of the window. The clock in the yard read 2.30. Surely Lord Delham should have returned by now.

'For this we must go back more than twenty years, to the Forty-Five.' Lord Rossleigh began. 'Sir Martyn had just attained his majority and come into his inheritance, but his lands in Yorkshire and Hertfordshire were not enough for him. His father had been a fervent supporter of King James and now Sir Martyn put on a white cockade and rode north to support Charles James Edward, the Young Pretender.'

Sir Martyn sighed. 'Is there a point to this fairy-tale, Rossleigh? It grows mighty tedious already.'

Lord Rossleigh kept his eyes fixed upon Sir Jonas.

'We come now to the point, sir, and also to a mystery. Perhaps Sir Martyn wanted to increase his power and influence with the Jacobites, or perhaps he merely fell in love with a pretty face. Whatever the reason, he courted a young heiress from a good Scottish family, Aileen MacCrae. Her father would not consent to the marriage, and urged them to wait until more peaceful times, but Pudsey was impatient and he ran off with Aileen and married her. We know that the northern rebellion failed, with bloody reprisals for the losers. When it became clear the cause was lost Pudsey slipped back to his Hertfordshire estates to lick his wounds. But he now had a problem. His wife's family had been discredited, stripped of lands and titles and the menfolk transported. The lady would no longer inherit a fortune and Pudsey badly needed one. So he decided to take a new wife.'

There was a stillness in the room. Sir Jonas was listening intently, and for all his nonchalant lounging, Sir Martyn's eyes were fixed on the earl.

'But how could he do that?' interposed Mr Crannock. 'He already had a wife.'

'Did he?' countered the earl. 'There was no written record. Remember that in those days it was enough for a couple to declare their vows to make the marriage binding. Pudsey decided to disown the lady, declaring to his friends in England that she had never been more than his mistress. Then he committed her to a sanctuary, an asylum for lunatics.'

Mrs Langridge gasped and Sir Jonas shifted in his seat. Only Sir Martyn remained unmoved.

'A fairy-tale, Rossleigh.'

'Many rebels fled abroad after the Forty-Five, and it was there that I first heard rumours that Pudsey had locked up a woman, some called her his mistress, others his wife. Since I returned to England four years ago I have been searching the asylums of England looking for this poor unfortunate.'

'But surely,' murmured Mrs Langridge, 'the lady's family would object. . . .'

'You forget, madam, the terrible vengeance meted out in Scotland at that time. Many families were destroyed, Aileen's menfolk had all been sent to the Indies and other members of her family turned off their land, the penalty for supporting the Pretender. Also, she was now hundreds of miles away from Scotland – how was her family to know what was happening in Hertfordshire?'

Sir Jonas sat forward, frowning slightly.

'Go on, my lord.'

'To continue: Sir Martyn had the woman locked away in a private asylum. Then, posing as a single man, he married Mary Garwood, a rich widow, somewhat older than himself, but with her fortune untrammelled by restrictions. He became a rich man. The only thing she couldn't give him was an heir. So when she died some twelve years ago he looked for another bride. This time he wanted birth and beauty as well as an unencumbered fortune. He found them all in my sister Susannah.'

Mrs Langridge looked up.

'But if his first wife was still alive. . . .'

'Exactly so, madam. We did not know it at the time, of course, but still my family did not favour the match. Pudsey persuaded Susannah to elope with him.'

Sir Martyn's sneering smile grew. He waved one white hand towards the earl.

'Finally, there is some truth in the tale, Sir Jonas.' He

addressed the magistrate. 'I confess I did run off with the lady; what else was I to do when her family would not countenance a marriage? The lady was of age, we were to be married by special licence. If all had gone well, she would have been very happy with me.'

'No one who knows your cruelty could imagine that!' retorted the earl.

'Yes, you were always against it, were you not, Rossleigh? You bragged you would see your sister dead before you allowed her to marry me, and you carried out that threat. You killed her, my lord.'

Amelia felt sick at heart as she looked at Lord Rossleigh, his lips narrowed and his face pale with anger. She wanted to run to him, to defend him, but she felt paralysed and unable to move. At last he spoke, his voice low.

'Yes, I have blamed myself for her death these dozen years. It was after all my pistol that she used to kill herself, but everything I have learned about you convinces me now that had she married you she would have suffered an even worse fate.'

'And is this your petty revenge, my lord?' Sir Martyn's words fell softly into the silence.

Sir Jonas cleared his throat. 'Lord Rossleigh, if you have no evidence to substantiate your claims—'

'I do, Sir Jonas. I have a statement from Sir Martyn's old valet, Graby, who accompanied him to Scotland and was a witness to the marriage. The old man was pensioned off some fifteen years since, but I traced him to a little village in Kent. He was an old man when we met, but his memory was as sharp as ever and he gave me a very detailed account of Pudsey's marriage to Aileen MacCrae.'

'And is this valet able to give his evidence in person?' enquired the magistrate, pressing the tips of his fingers together.

'Unfortunately not. Shortly after my visit the old man died, but I have here his sworn deposition, which he signed in his own hand, witnessed by his sister.'

The sound of a carriage pulling up in the yard made Lord Rossleigh pause and look up, but his brow darkened when he saw it was merely a farmer's gig.

Sir Martyn laughed softly.

'Hardly enough to hang a man, Rossleigh.'

The earl shrugged.

'Perhaps not. But this is.' He held up a small, leather-bound notebook. 'It is the valet's journal of his years with you. Daily notes on your ill-fated expedition to Scotland and your meetings with the supporters of Charles Stuart. Also, your marriage to Aileen MacCrae: names, dates and such detail as can be confirmed with a little investigation.'

Sir Martyn's eyes narrowed.

'Where did you get that?'

'Let us just say I acquired it.'

'But that's impossible – I burned it—'

'You burned one copy.'

Sir Martyn jumped up from his chair, an angry oath on his lips.

'Damn you, that's impossible!'

'Graby's conscience was troubling him and he gave me his signed deposition of your treasonous Jacobite activities, but I was surprised that he did not want immediate protection from me. What I did not know was that he was playing a double game. While he was in your service he had written a journal of everything he knew about you. This was to be his assurance that you would not harm him. However, I presume when you pensioned him off you knew nothing of the journal, or you would have been at pains to keep in touch with him. But after my first visit to Home End, Graby contacted you, did he not, offering to sell you his journal? I believe his plan was to take your money, as well as my reward and protection, thus gaining on all fronts. Your man Catling was seen in Home End on the evening I was visiting Graby, and when I had gone he forced his way in and stole the notebook before setting fire to the cottage. But the journal Catling brought you was only one copy. Graby thought to protect himself by making a second copy of the journal – and I now have that second copy, and Sir Jonas shall have it to make of it what he will – it will brand you a bigamist and a traitor.'

Sir Martyn spread his hands.

'Do you really think that after all this time anyone will be interested in this sordid little fairy-tale?'

'Oh I think they will. Graby was alive when I left him, as his sister will testify,' said Lord Rossleigh. 'And when Catling is arrested and identified as Graby's killer, I have no doubt that he will soon let it be known that he was working on your orders.' The earl glanced towards the magistrate. 'Catling has been with the family since he was a boy, and you will see from the journal that he, too, was a witness to that first, infamous marriage.'

Again Sir Martyn gave his sneering laugh.

'Pure conjecture, Rossleigh, and all your witnesses dead. Do you think anyone will want to stir it all up again?'

It seemed Lord Rossleigh did not hear him, for he was gazing out of the window at the coach that had just drawn up, but now he turned, the mocking light back in his eyes.

'But they are not all dead, Sir Martyn.' He paused as the door opened and Lord Delham walked in.

'Ah, Henry – in good time, sir. Is she here?' The young lord nodded. 'Good. Then may I present to you, Sir Jonas, the true Lady Pudsey.'

Chapter Twenty Two

A sudden murmur fluttered around the room and all eyes were fixed on the doorway. A thin, grey-haired woman in a faded dimity gown was led into the room by a plump nurse in brown bombazine, who patted her hand reassuringly. They were followed closely by a gentleman in a black frock-coat and brown bag-wig. 'May I also present to you Dr Harwood, whom I hired to examine my lady.'

'I know the doctor.' Sir Jonas nodded at him. 'Sir.'

'And also Mrs Killigrew,' continued the earl, acknowledging the nurse. 'She has acted as my lady's nurse and companion since she came into my care.'

The grey-haired lady had been gazing about her, looking around with blank, uninterested eyes until her gaze fell upon Sir Martyn, who had risen from his chair and was staring, ashen-faced, at the woman.

'M-Martyn? Martyn, my hinny, is that ye?' She pulled away from the nurse and ran forward. 'Och but ye have been a long while coming to me, laddie! You said I must hide, hide from the soldiers, or they would kill me, like they killed my mother and sisters, but I've been so lonely, sir. Why did ye not come to me?'

Sir Jonas stepped forward, saying gently, 'Madam, can you tell us your name?'

She gave him a dreamy look.

208

'My name, sir? Why, 'tis Lady Pudsey. Some of the servants still call me Miss MacCrae, but I scold them so, and tell them I am Lady Pudsey. I have his ring, look.' She held out one thin hand bearing a plain gold band, then turned again to Sir Martyn. 'I wish you'd tell them, my love, tell them to address me as my lady. Have ye come to take me home, hen? Have the soldiers gone now?'

'Mistress,' Sir Jonas spoke again. 'Mistress – what is this man to you?'

The pale eyes looked at him, a slight frown creasing her brow, then a wide smile spread over her features.

'Why, sir, I have told you, he is my husband!'

Sir Jonas turned to the doctor.

'Can this be true, Harwood?'

'I accompanied Lord Rossleigh and Lord Delham to the house of one Mr Jameson, where the earl – ah – *persuaded* Jameson to deliver the lady into my care. She has not deviated from her story, Sir Jonas. However, she has lived locked away for nearly twenty years. Who can tell the damage to her mind?'

'Of course she is out of her wits!' exclaimed Sir Martyn, very pale. 'Besides, if you believe everything Rossleigh has told you of me, would I have let this creature live if she had really been my wife?'

Sir Jonas looked at the earl.

'Well, Lord Rossleigh?'

He shrugged. 'Perhaps he truly loved her.'

A shudder of emotion flickered over Sir Martyn's face, but he said nothing. A short silence settled over the room, then Sir Jonas got to his feet.

'You say you have the valet's deposition, Lord Rossleigh?'

'I have, sir, and the journal. You will find Graby's sister has letters signed by the valet which will prove to you that these documents were indeed written by his own hand.' The earl

209

went to the table and began to tidy the papers with his good hand. 'If you have heard enough, Sir Jonas, I will have these delivered to your house.' He glanced towards Sir Martyn, who was still staring in horrified silence at the grey figure standing trance-like before him.

Amelia found herself close to tears. She gazed out of the deep bay window, blinking rapidly. Despite the horrific revelations within the room, the business of the inn carried on as normal. A farmer in brown homespun stood by his cart in one corner of the yard, a tankard in one hand, chatting idly with a porter while they watched the driver of a smart yellow and black travelling chaise bring his high-stepping team to a halt, the stable boys scrambling to catch the horses' heads. Behind her, she heard the earl murmur instructions and she turned in time to see the doctor and nurse gently guiding Aileen from the room.

'Infamous,' muttered Mr Crannock. 'To lock up a young woman, to deprive her of her freedom, of her rightful station—'

'Spare me your moralizing!' snapped Sir Martyn. 'She was well cared for – God knows I paid enough.' He turned away, scowling and went to stand before the window. After a moment he said, 'I will answer all your questions, Sir Jonas, but first, if I might step outside for a little fresh air?'

Silently the magistrate nodded. Sir Martyn turned and walked to the door.

'Wait!' Amelia was staring across the yard. There was something familiar about the diminutive figure that had just entered the yard. She was wearing a heavily veiled lilac bonnet, more suited to an elderly lady than the youthful figure nimbly climbing into the travelling chaise. Amelia jumped to her feet. 'No – stop him. His carriage is in the yard!'

Immediately Lord Delham stepped in front of the door, his

210

hand on his sword, while Lord Rossleigh pulled a small pistol from his sling and levelled it at Sir Martyn. He stopped, lifting his eyes to meet the earl's challenging stare, then with a shrug he turned away from the door.

'I think, my lord, you will find Miss Strickland waiting in that travelling carriage,' offered Amelia.

Lord Rossleigh raised his brows.

'Mr Crannock,' he said, 'perhaps you would be good enough to go and see. Go with him, Delham, Catling may be there.'

Amelia sank down again into her chair and moments later Mr Crannock returned, escorting the veiled lady. Lord Delham followed them into the room, shaking his head in answer to the earl's questioning glance.

'It is Sir Martyn's coachman, but he thinks the groom is still at the Bull.'

'Then we shall apprehend him there.' Sir Jonas beckoned the lady forward. 'Come in, madam, and put up your veil, if you please. You have nothing to fear.'

Two dainty hands in cream kid gloves lifted the lilac net to reveal Miss Strickland's heart-shaped countenance, her dark eyes wide with apprehension. She looked around the room, then towards Sir Martyn, who regarded her with indifference. Sir Jonas nodded and bent a fatherly eye upon Camilla.

'Well my dear, there is no need to be alarmed. Had you an assignation with Sir Martyn?' Camilla glanced at him, frowning slightly.

'Y-yes. He – he sent me a note.' She put up her chin, adding with a touch of defiance, 'We are going to Paris.'

'Paris!' declared Sir Jonas.

'Slipping out of the country, eh?' muttered Lord Delham. 'It would seem Pudsey knew the game was up.'

'And you would embroil this poor innocent child in your schemes.' Sir Jonas shook his head, looking more shocked at the thought than at all the revelations that had gone before.

'Shame on you, sir.'

Before Sir Martyn could reply there was a commotion outside the door and seconds later Mrs Strickland burst into the room.

'Where is my daughter?' She paused on the threshold, glancing swiftly around the room at the assembled company, then ran forward to envelope Camilla in a fierce embrace. 'Oh my poor child. Thank God you are safe! I set off as soon as I received your note, praying I would be in time to save you from a disastrous action.'

'Pretty words, madam,' sneered Sir Martyn, 'when you have lost no opportunity to throw the chit at my head.'

Sir Jonas looked at him with disgust.

'Enough, sir. It is time your contaminating presence was removed. I shall take you personally to the watch house.'

'The constable and two of the landlord's men are waiting outside to escort you, Sir Jonas,' said Lord Delham.

Mrs Strickland raised her head.

'Watch house?'

'Sir Martyn has to answer the most serious allegations, madam,' Sir Jonas told her. He put his hand on Sir Martyn's shoulder. 'If you are ready, sir.'

With a growl Sir Martyn shrugged him away.

'Ay, damn you. I'll come with you.'

Miss Strickland had been listening to this exchange wide-eyed, but she now broke free of her mama's embrace and ran towards Sir Martyn.

'I don't understand. What is happening, Sir Martyn? You promised to take me away.'

'Have you so little wit?' he sneered. 'Our elopement is not possible now, my dear.'

With a cry she cast herself upon his chest.

'Oh no, no, that cannot be. You promised.'

Sir Martyn looked down at her with contempt.

'Did I? Apologies then. You must find yourself another admirer. With your looks, my dear, it should not be difficult.' He grasped her shoulders and held her away from him. 'For heaven's sake, will you stop crying all over my waistcoat, girl!'

Mrs Strickland hurried forward to take Camilla in her arms again, her eyes snapping.

'How dare you treat my daughter thus! She is a gently born girl.'

'She has the soul of a strumpet,' retorted Sir Martyn, 'And you, madam, are no better, trying to sell her to the highest bidder.'

'Silence!' cried Sir Jonas. 'Sir, it is time you were gone.' He nodded to the earl. 'I will give orders that Catling is to be apprehended.'

With a nod to the company the magistrate escorted Sir Martyn from the room. Lord Delham closed the door behind them and turned to the earl.

'Well, we have done it. Well done, Ross. Will the charges hold, do you think?'

'Oh, little doubt of it, and I'm confident that Pudsey's groom will confess all to save his own skin, once he knows his master has been arrested.'

'Good. Then if you don't need me any longer, I'll be off. I want to find Isabelle and tell her the good news – she's a free woman now.'

Lord Rossleigh smiled.

'Yes. Take my curricle. If you hurry you might catch them before they leave for France.' He glanced at Amelia. 'You said they were heading south, my lady?'

'Plymouth.' She smiled at Lord Delham. 'I wish you luck, my lord, and God speed.'

He caught her hand and lifted it to his lips.

'Thank you, Lady Langridge.'

Her fingers grasped his.

'And – Mr Lyddon?'

'Have no fear, madam. If he loves her I will not come between them. God knows Issy deserves some little happiness now.' With a cheerful smile and a nod to the earl, Lord Delham departed.

Amelia sank back on to her chair, exhausted by the events of the afternoon. The clatter and shouts in the yard outside the window continued, but there was silence in the room, save for the occasional sob from Camilla as she sat on the settle with her mother's arms about her. Mrs Langridge rose and went across to her daughter.

'My poor child — you look worn out, let me take you home. . . .'

Mr Crannock stepped forward.

'I think first, madam, that we should acknowledge our gratitude to the earl for his part in protecting Lady Langridge.'

Mrs Langridge paused, saying a little impatiently, 'I am sure that is understood. . . .'

'And further,' Mr Crannock raised his voice slightly, 'to assure his lordship that he need not feel obliged to make reparation to the lady, with regard to her honour.' He shifted slightly as several pairs of eyes stared at him. 'We are all aware that because of the outrageous events of the past two days, the lady's reputation has been compromised, but I fully understand the circumstances, and although I think that Lady Langridge would have done better to return to Langridge Court with the rest of her party, there is no doubting that she acted from the noblest of motives, even if her judgement was misguided.'

Amelia drew in an indignant breath, but Mr Crannock did not notice. He clasped his hands behind his back as he took a few slow paces about the room, saying ponderously, 'It has long been my desire to ally myself with the family — indeed,

I think I can say that it was the wish of the late baron, your grandfather, was it not, Amelia? Despite this unfortunate occurrence, let me assure you, my dear, that I have no intention of withdrawing my suit. You may rest easy, my dear. I shall marry you, and relieve his lordship of any obligation he might feel in that quarter.'

Mr Crannock came to a stand before Lord Rossleigh and made him a slight bow. The earl raised his brows, and lifted his quizzing glass to stare at him.

'Edmund,' murmured Amelia in an awed voice, 'perhaps you have not properly understood. I rode into Bath sitting across the earl's saddle . . . *minus my petticoats.*'

'I'm afraid what you say is not quite true, my lady,' the earl corrected her. 'We had some of your petticoats – they were bound about my shoulder.'

Mr Crannock visibly shuddered at this and he frowned at the earl, but his lordship had turned away and was making for the door. Amelia watched him in dismay, biting her lip to prevent herself from calling out to him not to leave her. She found Mr Crannock was addressing her again.

'You must be aware that your conduct will give rise to much comment, madam. That is most unfortunate, but I understand that, and I think a protracted visit to the country would be beneficial, until the gossip dies down. And of course we must take care that in future your conduct is beyond reproach.'

Mrs Langridge drew herself up.

'I think that this should be discussed another time, Edmund,' she said, glancing at her daughter. 'We do not yet know what Lord Rossleigh's wishes may be on this matter.'

Mrs Strickland, listening intently to this interchange, decided to enter the lists. She had seen one suitor slip away and was determined to make a push to salvage something from the disaster.

'We can all guess that the earl would not wish to be coerced into marriage,' she declared.

'There is no question of coercion,' replied Mrs Langridge.

Mrs Strickland rose to her feet.

'I see your design, madam,' she said, her eyes kindling, 'You wish to secure Lord Rossleigh for your daughter. Well, it will not do! Accept Mr Crannock's offer with gratitude, ma'am and be thankful that she should come out of this with some shreds of her character still intact.'

'Oh, if we are to talk of characters,' retorted Mrs Langridge, bridling, 'perhaps I should remind you that it was *your* daughter who planned to run off with Sir Martyn, where there could be no *hope* of a marriage!'

Camilla, still seated on the settle, looked up at that.

'Sir Martyn would have married me,' she declared tearfully. 'He was going to take me to Paris until Parliament granted his divorce.'

Mrs Langridge gave her a pitying look.

'Well if you believed that, miss, you are a bigger ninny-hammer than I thought you.'

This was too much for Mrs Strickland, who immediately launched a verbal assault upon Mrs Langridge, reminding her of her goodness in offering to introduce Amelia into Society, listing the times she had gone out of her way to guide Amelia, who had proved to be a viper in her bosom, leading dearest Camilla astray with her hoydenish tricks. Mrs Langridge could not be expected to ignore this attack upon her only child, and it was not long before the two ladies were entered into a full-scale argument. Camilla sank back, crying noisily, and Mr Crannock stood looking on helplessly as the two matrons gave vent to their pent-up emotions. A light knocking on the door went unregarded and after a moment the earl's valet entered into the room and quietly requested Lady Langridge to step outside with him.

*

Pleased to have an excuse to leave the room, Amelia followed him quickly into the yard, where she found the earl waiting for her. He had put on his coat, but the left sleeve was empty and the coat was merely draped over the sling. He met her anxious glance with a reassuring smile that won an answering gleam from her own eyes.

'You are well out of it, my lord. The ladies are quickly reaching cap-pulling – when I left the room they were already dragging up every injustice they had suffered at each other's hands during their schooldays.'

'I thought it was moving that way.' He put a hand under her elbow and guided her towards the travelling chaise, where O'Brien had gone ahead to hold open the door.

Amelia hesitated, looking up at the earl with a slight frown.

'My lord?'

'Get in, my dear, and I will explain.'

'But – this is Sir Martyn's carriage.'

'I have – er – borrowed it,' murmured the earl, helping her up the steps.

'But why, sir?'

'To abduct you.'

She stopped, turning to laugh at him.

'Now you are being absurd!'

'Not at all.' He firmly propelled her up the steps into the carriage and jumped up behind her, wincing a little as he jarred his injured arm.

'Oh please be careful!' cried Amelia. 'I do think you should be resting, my lord, until your arm is properly healed.'

'It is no more than a scratch and will mend soon enough.'

Even as he spoke the steps were put up, O'Brien closed the door upon them and the carriage lurched forward, recalling

Amelia to her present situation.

'Where are you taking me?'

'To Chantry.'

'Wh-where?'

'My hunting-lodge, just north of Burford,'

'Burford! But – you cannot take me there!'

'I am afraid I must contradict you, my lady.'

'But – I have no maid with me – and no baggage!'

His eyes gleamed. 'I believe that is usually the case, in an abduction.'

She could not resist an answering smile, but shook her head at him.

'Pray be serious, my lord.'

The earl settled himself in the corner, stretching out his long legs.

'I was never more so. I decided to remove you from Crannock's presence before he realized that you were making may-game of him – or I planted him a facer.'

She chuckled.

'Poor Edmund, so pompous. I was never so cross with anyone in my life. But what he will say when he finds we are gone!'

'I neither know nor care. When you next meet him, my love, you will be Countess Rossleigh, and may even cut the acquaintance, if you so wish.'

There was silence. Amelia stared at him, the colour drained from her cheeks.

'G-good heavens, you are serious! I-I thought you were merely cross with Edmund, and that you were taking me back to Langridge Court.'

The earl smiled at her.

'No, my sweet idiot, I am taking you to Chantry, where I mean to keep you until I can arrange our wedding. O'Brien will escort your mama there to join us tomorrow – I have no doubt that she will come – and you will stay there until we are wed. The ceremony will be a very quiet affair, because of your recent bereavement.'

'Ross you cannot run away with me, my reputation will be ruined! Pray, sir, take me to Langridge Court and we can set off from there in the morning, with a chaperon.'

The earl merely smiled at her.

'You forget, sweet life, that your reputation is already ruined, and I am not giving Crannock or anyone else the chance to talk you out of marrying me.'

Amelia flushed slightly.

'Oh they could not do that, my lord, I promise you.' She hesitated, before casting a shy glance up at him. 'Do you – do you *truly* wish to many me?'

He sat up and reached out his good hand to grasp both of hers.

'My dearest love I do not think I could live without you now.'

A glow of happiness spread through Amelia, but before she could speak again the carriage's steady pace slowed and shouting could be heard from the road. The earl listened, frowning, then moved to the door.

'Wait here.'

He jumped down. The road was bounded on both sides by thick woodland through which the evening sunlight filtered to leave a dappled pattern on the ground. His lip curled as he saw the solitary rider blocking the road, his pistol aimed at the driver on the box.

'Pudsey. How melodramatic.' The earl glanced up at the roof of the coach where Catling, Sir Martyn's groom had scrambled up and was deftly binding up the driver and groom. 'How did you persuade Sir Jonas to let you go?'

'The old fool trusted me. Catling had come to the White Hart and seen what was afoot so he followed us, and at the right moment . . . ' Sir Martyn shrugged. 'Sir Jonas will have a sore head tomorrow.'

'And now you have come for your revenge on me.'

'On the contrary, dear fellow, I have come for my carriage. I am off to France – an Englishman can live very well in Paris, if he has friends, and believe me, I know some of the most influential men. And once there I shall track down my wife, the faithless jade! You still have my trunk with you and since I must fly the country it would be useful to take it with me.' He saw Amelia at the carriage window. 'Miss Langridge, pray step out and join the earl. My, my, have I perhaps stumbled upon an elopement?'

'Take the carriage and go,' retorted the earl.

Catling had climbed down from the coach and was brandishing his own pistol. Sir Martyn dismounted.

'What, and leave you here unharmed? Where is your sense of justice, Rossleigh? No, no, I am branded a traitor now, so what have I to lose by adding two more murders to my name? I shall kill you, Rossleigh, and your whore, but not until I have tried her for myself.'

He raised the pistol.

'Wait!' The earl stepped forward. 'Where is the enjoyment in shooting me, Pudsey? Would you not prefer to put your sword through my heart?' He grinned, and added softly, 'Or are you still afraid to face me, even when I have only one good arm?'

Sir Martyn frowned.

'I am not afraid of you.'

'My duelling swords are in the carriage. Untie my footman and he will find them for you.'

Sir Martyn laughed at that.

'Do you think me dull-witted, Rossleigh? Catling shall get them.'

Amelia stood beside the earl and restrained herself from

clutching his arm. Fear had weakened her knees but she steadied her breathing, praying that she would not faint. After what seemed like hours Catling jumped down from the carriage with a slim wooden box tucked under his arm. As he turned the case towards Sir Martyn and opened it, Amelia was reminded of a jeweller displaying his wares for a customer. She felt hysterical laughter welling up and bit her lip, determined not to lose control. Two shining small-swords lay on a bed of blue silk, their silver hilts gleaming in the evening sunlight. Sir Martyn picked up one of the swords and tested it, approving its fine balance in his hand.

'French,' murmured the earl. 'But to my own design.'

Sir Martyn lifted the sword and peered closely at the hilt. He glanced across at the earl.

'You have had it engraved – *Suzanne.*'

'For my sister Susannah. I had them made for only one purpose.'

Sir Martyn placed the sword back in the box and began to remove his coat.

'Very well, I will fight you, Rossleigh. How apt it will be to kill you with your own weapon.'

The earl did not answer. He turned to Lady Langridge and requested her assistance to remove his coat. As she did so he slipped her the little pistol that had been hidden in his sling.

'It is loaded,' he murmured. 'Only one shot – use it well.'

Swallowing hard, she folded the coat over her arm, keeping the pistol hidden beneath.

'Ross—'

He smiled, and lifted his hand to cup her cheek.

'Don't frown, dear heart,' he said lightly, 'I detest it when you frown.'

Sir Martyn had already picked up a sword and was waiting on the road. Lord Rossleigh walked towards him, taking the remaining small-sword from the box as he passed Catling.

221

'My style may be a little impaired by the bandages, Pudsey, but I am sure you will forgive that'

Sir Martyn lifted his sword in salute.

'*En garde.*'

Amelia jumped as the swords clashed together, the ringing of the steel echoing through the trees. Sir Martyn was the bigger of the two men, but he was surprisingly agile as he went in for the attack. His sword cut through the air and he skipped forward, pushing his opponent into the defensive, but the earl parried every stroke while he danced nimbly away from the flashing blade. Back and forth they moved through the dappled sunlight, the earl's movements restricted by the sling on his left arm. He deflected a thrust at the heart and replied with a furious attack of his own which pushed Sir Martyn back until he lost his footing. As the big man went down on one knee Lord Rossleigh jumped back and tore off the sling. Then Sir Martyn was up again, and to the scrape and ring of the blades was added the grunts of the two men. Amelia could not look away. Her heart stopped when Sir Martyn lunged again but Rossleigh was too quick for him, parrying the blade with a reckless laugh. She saw a dark stain on the earl's left arm and realized in dismay that the pistol wound had started bleeding again. If Rossleigh was aware of it he gave no sign, but fought on with his teeth bared in a wicked smile, taunting Sir Martyn to attack. Both men were sweating, but Amelia thought that Sir Martyn looked the more exhausted, his face almost purple with rage and exertion. He launched himself once more at the earl, his blade twisting and turning so fast that Amelia did not know how Rossleigh could ever defend himself, but each time steel met steel until finally Sir Martyn gave a roar of rage and swept the earl's sword aside, following up with a savage thrust. The point was aimed at the earl's heart, but Rossleigh neatly sidestepped. The thrust went wide, but the momentum of Sir Martyn's lunging movement carried him forcefully on to the earl's waiting sword.

Amelia gasped. Where all had been noise and movement there was now a silent tableau. Sir Martyn looked down at the blade embedded beneath his breastbone, frowning a little at the red stain that was spreading over his waistcoat. Lord Rossleigh, breathing heavily, stepped back and pulled out his sword. After a moment Sir Martyn's knees buckled and he fell silently to the ground.

Amelia bit her lip, fighting down a feeling of nausea that had swept over her. She wanted to run to the earl but her legs would not obey her and she found herself trembling. At that moment she caught a movement to one side of her and turned to see the groom Catling taking aim at the earl. With a cry of alarm she fired the little pistol. The bullet whistled past the groom's ear and he jumped back as he fired, his shot burying itself harmlessly in a tree.

After assuring himself that Sir Martyn was dead, Lord Rossleigh turned towards the groom, levelling the bloody tip of his sword at him.

'If you know what's good for you, you will climb up and untie my men. And don't think of running off, I still have a loaded carriage pistol that would make short work of you.'

White-faced, Catling did as he was bid while the earl scooped up the discarded sling with his sword and proceeded to clean the blade. He cast a swift glance at Amelia.

'When we get to Chantry, my lady, I will give you some lessons in marksmanship.'

She averted her eyes from the body on the road.

'But surely we should return to Bath.'

'No. My footman will take Sir Martyn's horse and escort Catling to the watch house – we'll bind his hands before they go so that he can do no more mischief. *We* are going on to Chantry.'

He helped her into the coach. Amelia found that she was shaking, and she leaned back against the squabs, watching in a detached manner as Catling was tied to his horse and led away by the earl's footman. By the time the earl climbed into the coach she had recovered her wits sufficiently to speak.

'B-but what about Sir Martyn?'

'Gad, my lady you don't want to take him with us?' He saw her distress and dropped the bantering tone. 'He is dead, Amelia. Sir Jonas will send a party of men to collect the body. You and I have done enough for today.'

'But. . . .'

He held up his hand.

'Madam, that is my last word on it! Now, I believe I need your assistance to bandage up my arm again.'

At once she was all concern.

'Oh my dear sir, is it still bleeding? Does it hurt dreadfully?'

The earl leaned back against the squabs and looked at her, his blue eyes glinting.

'I fear, madam, that we must again make use of your petticoats!'